P9-ECA-278

Could I fall in love with a man such as Charles Pierce? He is handsome, charming, rich....Any girl would be lucky to have him interested in her, yet.... Amanda's thoughts faltered, and Luke's face popped into her head. *What about Luke?* One man gave her goose bumps, the other a warm feeling in her chest. Luke was a good, respectable, God-fearing man. While Charles's reputation was questionable, it seemed to make him more exciting. Amanda had never known a man such as Charles.

Which man, if either, could Amanda Barker trust with her heart?

Also by Barbara Masci

Forbidden Legacy Set in the 1800s, this fascinating story follows Sarah Clarke, who arrives by stagecoach to claim a Texas cattle ranch she inherited from her grandfather. However, the foreman, a half-breed called Storm, also claims ownership. Who has the legal right to the Arrow C ranch?

CAPTURED
HEART

BY Barbara Masci.
Forbidden Legacy
Captured Heart

CAPTURED
HEART
BARBARA
A·MASCI

Power Books

Fleming H. Revell Company
Old Tappan, New Jersey

Scripture quotations in this volume are from the King James Version of the Bible.

Library of Congress Cataloging-in-Publication Data

Masci, Barbara.
    Captured Heart / Barbara Masci.
        p.   cm.
    ISBN 0-8007-5331-3
    I. Title.
    PS3563.A7817C3   1989
    813′.54—dc20   89-34518
                                                                                                 CIP

All rights reserved. No part of this publication may be reproduced, stored in a retrieval system, or transmitted in any form or by any means—electronic, mechanical, photocopy, recording or any other—except for brief quotations in printed reviews, without the prior permission of the publisher.

Copyright © 1989 by Barbara Masci
Published by the Fleming H. Revell Company
Old Tappan, New Jersey 07675
Printed in the United States of America

CAPTURED HEART

1

*T*he tender tiptoeing of the raindrops soon began to sound like grains of rice bombarding the wagon's tightly stretched canvas top.

Their sound pulled Amanda Barker from her dazed stupor. Lying upon her bedroll, she focused her swollen, red-rimmed eyes on the indentations the torrents of rain momentarily imprinted on the cloth roof as the early-morning storm raged.

"Angels' tears," she spat. Gramma Hurley had always said that at rainy funerals.

Amanda pounded her pillow. "Let them cry!" Bitterness hid her beauty as she buried her fists into the pillow again.

"Why did you let this happen, God? Why?" Her voice grew louder as she choked on her words. "Why take Mama? Why Pa? Why Phillip? Why Hazel Jane?" She gazed upward, suddenly puzzled, "And why not me?" Amanda began to tremble and her face wrinkled as if she might cry, yet no tears fell. "God, please take me too; I just can't bear it without them!"

No more tears could be squeezed from her large, green eyes; they'd been used up hours ago. Only the telltale signs revealed the grief of the past forty-eight hours: her swollen, raw eyelids and bright-red nose.

As if finally answering an inner call, she jumped up and nimbly began scooping up her family's personal belongings. Tossing them recklessly into a trunk, she stopped now and then to fondle some beloved possession. Pa's watch, Mama's golden locket, Hazel Jane's rag doll, and even Phillip's handmade fishing pole. She recalled the first catch on the now-mangled hook, hanging from tangled, worn string.

She tossed it into the trunk with a scowl. *Useless, sentimental, heart-tugging objects—that's all they are! I must put them away, out of sight, if I want to survive and carry out our dream of reaching California.* The past lay behind her; they were dead. Cholera had beaten them, but it hadn't beaten her. She'd make it on her own. *They would have wanted that.*

Aunt Hattie was expecting them in San Francisco. Poor Aunt Hattie—wait until she found out the two of them were now all that remained of the Homer Barker family, formerly of Springview, Ohio.

Amanda scanned the wagon by the dim light of the kerosene lamp. Had she missed anything? Something shiny gleamed at her from a pocket sewed into the side of the wagon cloth. She reached for it. The family portrait. Drawing her arm back, she prepared to toss it into the now heaping-full trunk, but caught herself. Instead, she pressed the framed picture to her breast until its sharp corner drew blood from her upper arm. Drawing the photograph back, she held it before her and studied it with a grimace.

If only she could go back to that day. How happy they'd

been. Of course, you'd never guess that by the stern-looking faces. Only five-year-old Hazel Jane smiled. They all should have. Only her little sister looked her natural self.

She touched the image of her pa gently. He stood proudly behind his seated wife, one hand on his watch chain, the other resting fondly on lovely Anna Barker's shoulder. Seated at Mama's feet, Hazel Jane grinned brightly, so plump, rosy, and full of life.

Phillip stood arrogantly behind Amanda's chair, trying to imitate Pa and look well beyond his fifteen years. He didn't look himself without his seldom-missing, boyish smile.

Oh, she thought, *why do families pose so somberly?* Even her own image frowned back at her. Why had she pinned up her long, dark, thick hair? She remembered promising herself after first viewing the photograph never to wear her hair up again and to smile more.

Now, here she sat, sure she'd never want to smile again. Here, miles from Ohio, miles from Aunt Hattie, miles from anywhere—all alone.

Getting up, she peeked out the back of the wagon. The rain had stopped, but the dawn refused to break through the still-cloudy skies. *Well,* she thought, *if the train moves today, at least there won't be that dratted dust!* The rain had solved that problem.

Will the train move today? she wondered. It had been halted for three days. Too many passengers had ailed with cholera. Too many burials. Too many grieving families; those left on the train had to recuperate.

She pulled her head back into the wagon and began to neaten it for travel. If they did move today, she must be prepared to drive the team. Could she do it? She'd sat beside Pa and watched him steer the oxen. How difficult could it be? She must. She had no choice.

Jumping from the rear of the wagon, she yanked the

bucket from its hook and swung it over her shoulder. She'd need fresh water to wash. Perhaps she'd feel better, cleaned up.

Amanda headed down the path, made by numerous other wagon-train campers in the last few years, to the banks of the Platte River. Purposefully she held her head high so as not to see the four fresh graves along the side of the trail. There had been two new ones added, she'd heard, but she didn't want to see them. *At least they weren't alone,* she thought. Just last week Lulu Beecham and Mama had laughed at Amanda's burnt biscuits; now they were eternal neighbors. The other grave held Lulu's daughter, Emily.

Amanda knelt by the shore and lowered her bucket. She gasped and jumped up as a large figure reflected in the water beside her.

"Oh, Captain Larsen!"

The short, spry, middle-aged man spoke kindly, but as brusquely as ever. "Sorry to alarm you, my dear, but ve must talk right avay." His Swedish accent was only slight but clearly definable on *w*s.

"As you please, sir," Amanda mumbled politely, her mind blank yet curious. "Can we speak here, or would you like to come back to my wagon?"

"Here is fine," he replied. "I have a job to do and vill come right to the point. Vithout a man to head your vagon, I'm afraid you'll have to leave the train." His blue eyes, she noticed, looked past her as he spoke, as if unable to meet hers.

"L-leave? Leave the wagon train?" She felt her knees tremble. "Where shall I go? Will you just leave me here alone?" Her head throbbed; she began to feel dizzy.

When Amanda next opened her eyes, she lay in her own wagon, upon her mat, looking up into Mr. Larsen's bright-blue eyes and a pair of strange hazel ones.

"Are you all right, Miss Barker?"

"I guess so," she answered Larsen but continued to stare into the stranger's face.

The hazel-eyed stranger spoke, "Lucky I happened by at just that moment, or you'd have hurt yourself falling backwards like that."

Amanda fumbled for words of explanation, her eyes flitting from one man to the other for help.

"The young lady," Larsen explained, "has had some tough luck." He shifted his weight uncomfortably. "Cholera took her whole family in just three days. I vas just explaining to her vhy she'd have to leave the train."

"I see," the stranger whispered compassionately. "May I have a few words with her alone?"

Larsen looked about uncomfortably.

"I mean," the young man reddened, "outside the wagon, of course."

He asked Amanda, "Are you up to a valk vith him?"

Amanda looked from one to the other, still confused.

The young man whispered hoarsely to Larsen. "Maybe you should introduce us. . . ."

"Of course," he shook his white head, "How ignorant of me! Miss Amanda Barker, this is Mr. Lucas Vest. He's been hired by me as a trail hand. He has no vagon, just a horse and bedroll, but he's a hard vorker, and I'm mighty glad to have him aboard."

"My friends call me Luke," he began after settling her comfortably beside himself on a dead log near the river. "The reason I wanted a word with you is—" He picked up a flat stone and played with it as he spoke. "I think I know how you must feel, for I've recently lost a loved one, too. Your pain must be four times as sharp as mine. And mine is plenty sharp!"

When Amanda didn't answer, but continued to stare at him, he made a hasty confession. "I also overheard you early this morning, blaming God, and that troubles me greatly."

Amanda's look was curious and a bit angry. "You . . ., you . . ., what?"

"I heard you refer to the rain as angels' tears and ask God why He took away your family. I wasn't eavesdropping—you were quite loud. I was on my way to the river and passed your wagon. Couldn't help hearing. . . ."

Amanda turned away, half embarrassed, half angry at having her private moment invaded by this stranger.

"Don't blame God, Miss Barker." He touched her arm gently. "Blaming causes bitterness. Bitterness grows like weeds and smothers flowers—like you."

Amanda examined him. Was he mocking or sincere? His eyes held hers evenly.

Luke continued, "If we weed the garden and kill the ugly, deadly weeds, the flowers live, thrive, and are worthy of the beauty God gave them."

He took his hand from her arm and toyed with the stone again before hurling it into the river at an angle that amused Amanda, despite her grief. The stone skipped across the water four or five times before neatly sliding into its depths.

As they stared after the stone, he said, "You are just like a flower. Don't let the weeds, bitterness, kill your beauty, your vitality and spirit."

Amanda studied his sensitive face. If his nose were not a bit too long, he would be handsome. Even the barely noticeable scar between his sandy colored hair and shaggy eyebrows couldn't detract from his pleasing appearance. Only his nose and extreme ruggedness stopped her from calling him classically handsome.

He was definitely likable, though. *The type of man a woman feels like mothering,* she thought. *Probably because of the boyish way he scoops his hair from his eyes with a whisk of his hand or the way he squints when unsure of the effect of his words.* But why did she feel as if she'd known him for years, when they'd just met? *Of course,* she decided, *he reminds me of Phillip.* Though well over twenty, this man before her had all Phillip's boyish qualities.

"Thank you for talking to me," she said at last. "It has all happened so fast—I'm so confused. I just buried my family, and now I'm told to leave the train. Where shall I go? Will they just leave me here?" She felt a tear slip from one eye and was genuinely surprised when he caught it with his rough yet gentle finger.

"Of course not," he said with tender gruffness. "Larsen isn't the most tactful fellow." Again Luke hesitated and squinted boyishly. "Actually, there are two choices open to you. If another family takes you in, you may stay. Otherwise, you'll be escorted, by me or Griff, to the nearest town. If there is a financial need, everyone in the train pitches in. You'd never be just left on your own; I promise you that."

Amanda let out a breath of relief and relaxed somewhat.

"In fact . . .," he jumped up with beaming eyes.

There, Amanda noted, *just like Phillip! So enthusiastic!* Her heart tugged for this new friend and for her beloved brother. She listened attentively to his idea.

"I'll spread the word around the train that you need a family. Perhaps there's someone needing a good pair of female hands."

"You think they'd take me in?" she asked, wide-eyed.

"It's worth a try."

"Thank you, Mr. West," she replied, twisting her wrinkled handkerchief.

"Luke," he insisted.

"Amanda," she whispered back.

Luke turned and sped down the path excitedly, but turned to wave and smile—that irresistible Phillip-like smile.

In the morning, word passed quickly from wagon to wagon that the train would move out in one hour. Amanda panicked once again. Could she manage the oxen team? Would they allow her to drive? Her heart skipped a beat— her oxen weren't even harnessed to the wagon! She'd never watched Pa or Phillip do that! She doubted she could even lift the heavy halters. Whatever would she do? She sat upon her bedroll, buried her face in her hands, and began to cry softly.

2

*A*s Amanda wept, she felt the wagon shift slightly. Had she imagined it? No. There, it moved again. The wagon was being lightly jostled. She jumped to her feet and dashed to the back opening. She saw nothing unusual, but on her way to the front flap, she recognized a familiar mixture of leather and metal sounds, reminding her of Pa.

Opening the front flap, behind the driver's bench, she saw Luke West bent over her oxen, harnessing them. He glanced up and smiled. 'Hope you don't mind me for company, 'cause Larsen gave me permission to drive for you today.'

Amanda guessed her beaming smile was all he needed for an answer, for he turned back to his chore.

Just as the lead wagons began to roll, Amanda glanced quickly toward the graves. A panicky feeling enveloped her. How strange it felt to leave her family behind. She gasped as she suddenly noticed the graves had changed. Each mound had a cross upon it, made from white rocks.

How beautiful! How thoughtful of someone! Tears she'd thought long dried up began to flow freely again.

"Go quickly," Luke urged, offering her his hand. "Say farewell—not good-bye. You *will* see them again." He glanced upward meaningfully.

She grasped his hand, jumped down, started to dart away, but stopped short and gazed up at him with wonder. "The crosses—did you . . . ?"

He nodded.

"Oh, thank you!" she cried tearfully before dashing the few feet to say farewell to her family.

That morning they continued along the much-traveled trail west, always within sight of the Platte River.

They passed many graves that day—too many for Amanda to count. It was sad yet comforting to know others shared her grief. While none of the graves they passed that day had beautiful white crosses laid in stone, some had boards propped up on them, giving the buried's name, origin, and cause of death. Most read *cholera*.

Amanda rubbed her stomach as a hunger pang nudged her. She hadn't eaten breakfast. When would they stop for lunch? Would she hear of someone who would be willing to take her in? Or would she be forced to leave the train? She rubbed her temples. If only she could pray. Why had God let her down? Hadn't she always gone to Sunday services? Hadn't she always prayed and thanked Him for everything? Why hadn't He listened to her plea for her family?

Luke's company comforted and reassured her, though they had little chance to talk. Driving on the wet and sandy trail took all his attention. The train noises also made conversation difficult: Babies cried; dogs barked; children ran beside wagons, calling out; and men shouted orders.

Once that morning they met a lone rider heading back to

Missouri. He'd told members of their train he'd lost his family to cholera.

When they stopped for lunch—bread and cold coffee— she confronted Luke about her position on the train.

"Well," he squinted uncomfortably, "we haven't had much response yet, but I'm sure we will. A few families seemed interested, but nothing definite yet."

"Then you think a family will take me in?"

"Where's your faith?" he asked, cuffing her chin lightly.

"Are you a preacher or something?" she asked.

"No. Why?"

"You sound like one."

"I read my Bible, but I'm no preacher. My brother Edward is. I didn't know what I was going to say yesterday to comfort you; I just asked God to give me the right words."

"You can do that? Ask for something like that and get it so quickly?"

"Sure, once you know Him."

"Anything?"

"No."

"Why not anything?"

"Anything isn't always good for us or what He wants for us."

"Then, if you had prayed for my family, they still would have died?"

"If it was God's will, yes."

"Is that fair?" she asked, looking up at him, tilting her head.

"Why do you think death is a bad thing? If they are with Him, perhaps they are the fortunate ones, and you are the one who has the 'bad' outcome."

"So you don't pray for people not to die?"

"No, I ask that if it be His will, to let them live; if not, then to take them peacefully and painlessly," he explained

"I come from a praying family, too. We all loved God and lived for Him. Yet when I needed Him most, He didn't hear me. I'll never pray again. Mama prayed, Pa prayed . . ., yet they all died. Why did God turn His back on us when we needed Him most?" she asked, briskly wiping tears from her cheeks.

"I wish Edward were here." Luke scooped his hair from his eyes. "I don't know what to say, Amanda. There are so many things we don't understand about God and the way He operates. Someday we'll know all the answers."

"Your words are comforting, but please try to under¯ stand. I feel as though God has forsaken me. Maybe I just need time. You made me feel so much better yesterday," she added.

"I did?"

"Very much so. Especially when you talked about weeds and flowers. Pa always called me his little flower." She smiled, remembering. "And Phillip used to tease by saying, 'Ya mean weed, don't ya, Pa?' "

Luke laughed. "Sounds familiar. I have four brothers and four sisters—well, three now," he saddened as he corrected himself.

"I'm sorry. Was it a sister, then, whom you spoke of yesterday when you said you'd recently lost a loved one, too?"

He nodded.

Amanda wished she could feel sympathy for this young man and his recent loss, but he'd only lost one sister. She'd lost her whole family

They talked lightly as they finished their meal. She cleared away the food and put things away, while Luke prepared for driving again

As she began to step down from the wagon, she hesitated at the sound of voices It was Luke and Captain Larsen

"No. Today only. Tomorrow she either leaves the train or goes vith another family. I can't spare you. Griff is complaining about scouting alone, vith Indians starting to show up. I hired you as a hand, remember?" Larsen's voice was shrill with anger.

"I know, but I may need more time. I'm having trouble finding a family for her."

"Vhy is that?" Larsen demanded.

"Two reasons. First, some are afraid she might carry cholera to their families. Then—you won't believe this— some of the women don't want her because she is too attractive. They are worried about their husbands and sons—well, you know   "

Amanda couldn't believe her ears! *Too attractive? Me?* She looked down at her slim figure clothed in a blue-and-white gingham dress and blue apron. She'd thought herself plain Touching her head, she felt her long, thick, almost black hair, stuffed recklessly inside her blue bonnet. A mess. *Who would think me attractive?*

The only part of herself she knew to be truly attractive were her eyes. Like her mother's, they were emerald green, almond shaped, and trimmed with thick, dark lashes.

Amanda strained to hear more but only heard Larsen repeat as he stormed away, "Only for today you drive her vagon." Amanda buried her face with her hands. Her head throbbed. She had but one day to find a family to take her in, and from what she'd just heard, her chances were slim

To burn off frustration, Amanda walked the whole afternoon, trying to think of what she should do. Use what money Pa had left her and return to Ohio? Stay at the nearest town and begin a new life? Wire Aunt Hattie in San Francisco? Give up or fight is what it amounted to She recalled Pa's excitement the day he came home and announced his plans to sell everything and go west. "Opportunity of a lifetime," he'd ranted. Amanda kicked a large pebble from her path and decided to fight. She'd make it to California and Aunt Hattie, if it took her whole lifetime to do it.

At dusk they made camp, still along the Platte River, at a place called Courthouse Rock. Luke disappeared to help the men settle the animals for the night, leaving Amanda alone to cook her own supper.

How she dreaded dragging out food, dishes, and cookware just for herself. Even building a fire for one person seemed a waste. She decided on dried apples and bread again. This time she added some hard cheese Mama had wrapped tightly and packed at the very bottom of the food barrel. She scraped the mold from the top and found it tastier than when she and Mama had first made it.

As she put the few things away she smelled the food of the nearby fires, heard laughter, the stories   How she missed her family!

"Miss Barker!" someone yelled, breaking into her thoughts. "Miss Barker!" a male voice sounded again, coming from the rear of the wagon.

Sticking her head out of the oval opening, she was stunned to see a well-dressed man of about thirty standing with hat in hand.

"Yes?" she asked curiously. She started to climb down from the wagon, and his hand shot out to assist her. It felt warm, friendly, and secure.

"I'm Charles Pierce, and I heard you are in need of a family. I am in need of someone to help my mother nurse my sister."

"You spoke to Luke West?" she asked.

"Who? No. I heard from the Elliotts, who heard of it from

the Simpsons." He laughed, blue eyes twinkling. "Word travels faster than we do, here on the trail!"

About to smile, Amanda caught herself. *Careful. What would Mama do next?*

"How many in your party, Mr. Pierce?"

"Just myself, my mother, and my sister, who is seriously ill. She needs much care, I'm afraid."

"Cholera?" She said the word fearfully.

"No—" he blurted quickly, then, "we don't know; aren't sure. At least we don't think it's cholera." He looked Amanda up and down appraisingly and added. "You are perfect."

"I beg your pardon, sir?"

"I mean, you look healthy and strong. We need someone who can lift Sis and be available whenever we have need.

Now this man is handsome! Amanda thought. But he dressed too fancily for the wagon train. None of the other men wore neatly pressed trousers with a white shirt— starched and pressed. She could also tell from his complexion that he was not an outdoorsman, for his skin lacked the tanned, weathered look of Luke and most of the other men

"I would contribute my wagon and stores to yours," she said in a businesslike tone, "and work as any family member. Not slave, Mr. Pierce, just do my share. Understood?"

"Perfectly."

"When would you like me to join your group?"

"Tonight. You can continue sleeping in your wagon we'll just park it behind ours. I brought a man along to drive my team, so I can drive your wagon—if he'll teach me " he laughed.

She'd guessed right. Mr. Pierce was a city gentleman. While driving a team was not his usual sport, he was willing to learn. She admired that and returned his smile

*   *   *

Amanda stood, stunned, when she was introduced to Charles's mother. A most unusual woman, unlike what she had envisioned a city gentleman's mother to be, from her dyed red hair to her course, brassy speech. Her dress appeared flashy and bright compared with the other women's on the train. Yet she seemed friendly, and Amanda was glad to have found a family.

"My daughter's real sick," explained Mrs. Pierce. "Don't reckon it's too serious; just don't cotton to travelin' I guess."

"It's not the cholera, is it Mrs. P-p—" Amanda began.

"Now don't you 'Mrs. Pierce' me!" she laughed. "Makes me feel like a stranger. We're family now. You just call me 'Ma.' "

"M-ma?"

"My real name's Helen, but everyone calls me 'Ma.' No, she don't have the cholera. I'm sure she'll be right as rain soon's we get to Frisco."

Amanda thought it strange neither she nor her son had mentioned the poor girl's name.

"What is your daughter's name?"

"Didn't Charles tell you?"

"No, he never did say."

"Louise," she said finally. "Her name is Louise."

"Will I get to meet her soon?"

"Tomorrow. She's abed for the night already."

Amanda shrugged, said good night, and turned toward her wagon, which was now behind the Pierces'.

"Nice meeting you, honey. See you in the morning," Helen called after her.

As she opened the rear flap to her wagon, Luke strode by and offered his hand. Once inside, she stuck her head out the back and smiled.

"Heard you found a family," he said flatly.

"Isn't it wonderful? Now I can stay with the train and keep my wagon, too!" she exclaimed.

"I'm happy for you," he said, not sounding it

"Is something wrong?" Amanda couldn't see clearly in the dark, but she was sure he was squinting.

"Be careful, Amanda. That family is strange

Strange? Amanda thought, as she curled up in her bedroll. Yes. Luke was right, they were a strange family. But harmless. Why had he sounded so fearful on her behalf? Why hadn't he been happy for her? Before she could ask herself anything more, she fell fast asleep.

In the morning, Amanda and Ma worked together on breakfast of pancakes and oatmeal. After they'd eaten, Ma prepared a bowl of oatmeal for Louise.

"C'mon, honey," she called. "You can help me feed Louise."

Amanda climbed into the Pierce's wagon behind Ma. Adjusting her eyes to the darkness of the wagon, it was moments before she made out the figure of Louise. Upon her bedroll, she lay in a fetal position. Amanda moved closer. While her brown hair was snarled and matted from thrashing, Amanda recognized that, despite her illness, Louise was a very handsome woman.

As she approached, Louise looked up at her anxiously with wide, fearful brown eyes.

"Hello, Louise." Amanda felt the need to whisper.

The young woman stared up at her and began moving her mouth excitedly, but no sounds could be heard. Ma immediately took charge.

"Calm down, Louise. This is Amanda. We've adopted her. I can see it's time for your medicine. Now, now be still," Helen Pierce held down Louise's now thrashing arms. Yet the whole time her eyes never left Amanda's.

Ma carefully measured a brown liquid into the oatmeal and force-fed the girl.

Amanda watched carefully, lest she be expected to serve the next meal. Something in Louise's eyes and the way they clung to her own haunted Amanda long after the girl had fallen asleep and she trudged beside her wagon. What had Louise's desperate look meant? Was Louise not just ill, but demented, and were the Pierces too proud to admit it? Something bothered Amanda. Had the look been a silent cry for help? A young, mentally deficient young girl's frantic crazed look? Or simply that of an ill girl under medication? Surely that was it. Perhaps Luke's warning had fed her imagination. Yet the feeling stayed with her all day.

3

*A*manda saw little of Luke except when she went to her wagon each evening before bed. He always seemed to come out of nowhere to exchange a few words and say good night. Charles now drove her wagon, and sometimes, rather than walk, she'd sit beside him. After a few days of traveling with Charles and Ma, they fell into a congenial pattern. Ma and Amanda took turns feeding Louise and shared all the other duties. Everyone got along, and Amanda began to settle into a pleasant routine. Yet Amanda felt uncomfortable about Louise and her frantic, crazed look. The better she became acquainted with Ma, the more she became suspicious. Not that she didn't trust Ma; they got along fine, and Amanda liked the woman despite her brashness. She just didn't fit the part of Charles's mother. Charles was a city gentleman. Helen was neither a city woman nor a lady

One evening, after she'd been traveling with the Pierces for a week, Charles walked her back to her wagon.

"Is everything working out to your satisfaction?" he asked. "Are you and Ma getting along?"

"Everything is fine and working far better than I'd expected." Amanda looked up at him in the moonlight and remarked to herself for the millionth time how handsome he was.

"Ma thinks the world of you," Charles said. "She agrees that you are perfect for us."

"Ma is wonderful. She isn't your real mother, is she?" Amanda held her breath after impulsively asking such a personal question. Had she any right to ask that? He was hesitating. Would he be angry? Would he answer? she wondered.

"No, of course not." He half chuckled. "But I feared telling you at the time, because you'd refuse to join us unless we were a proper family. Helen is *Ma* to everyone," he said, taking her hand. "So I wasn't really fibbing, just stretching the truth a bit. Will you forgive me?" he asked charmingly.

"Of course," she answered, very aware of her hand in his. "I know how endearing Helen can be. But why are you two traveling together? You seem so different, not at all an even match." As Amanda asked she again feared overstepping her bounds by being too inquisitive. "If you don't mind my prying," she amended.

"Not at all. Helen and I are business partners. I run a hotel in San Francisco, and she handles the female employees while I concentrate on the administrative and financial areas."

"Hotel? How interesting. Are the female employees maids or something?"

"Some, yes. Ah-h, Amanda, I must confess my hotel does a bit of gambling. I'm sure you don't approve, but it's very popular there, and business is booming. Some of the girls run the games, some dance and sing—that sort of thing. Are you shocked with us now?" he asked with uncertainty.

"A tavern with dancing girls?" she asked with widened eyes.

"Tavern?" He chuckled. "Absolutely not. My establishment is one of the finest this side of the Mississippi. The hotel is exclusive, with plush carpeting, crystal chandeliers, elegant furniture, and velvety wallpapers from Europe." He smiled and winked, adding in a whisper, "And the dancers are performers—artists, I assure you, not at all what you think."

Amanda continued to look at him suspiciously.

He smiled. "I provide good jobs to young women in need, and they love the work they do. Everyone has a good time. You must visit us when we get to Frisco. The hotel name is the *Golden Palace*."

"I guess," Amanda thought out her words carefully, "San Francisco is much different from Springview, Ohio. But why did you come back east?"

"To get Louise. Ma missed her."

"Will she work at the Golden Palace also?"

"We promised her she could."

"I hope she feels better soon," Amanda offered.

"I'm sure it's just the traveling that doesn't agree with her." He squeezed her hand lightly before releasing it. "And speaking of traveling, I have a few other wagons going west up ahead and must ride ahead to check on them. Ma knows how to drive the team, so you shouldn't miss me much." He laughed.

"More wagons? But why?" she asked.

"Supplies. There are so many things not available out west. So as long as we were returning with Louise, we decided to bring out more luxuries. This time I brought enough to sell; should turn a nice profit."

"How far ahead are they?" she asked.

"I have five other wagons, each in a different train. We did that so that if anything happened to one train the others would still get through."

"How long will you be gone?"

"Just a few days."

She looked up at his handsome, smiling face, with the square jaw and even, white teeth, and knew she'd miss him. "Are you sure Ma can handle the team?"

"Sure. She's a tough one." He cuffed her chin. "I'll miss you," he said quickly, dropping a kiss upon her forehead and disappearing into the night.

Amanda breathed deeply. How did she feel about Charles Pierce? He was handsome, charming, and always left her a bit shaken by his charisma. She leaned her head back against the wagon and relived the brief kiss he'd planted on her forehead. Just sisterly affection? She wondered. Would he miss her? Would she miss him?

"I don't think he's worth that dreamy look."

Amanda jumped. "Luke! I didn't know you were here!" Amanda knew she blushed at Luke's having caught her mooning over Charles.

"I'm sure you didn't." Roughly he dug his knife into a nearby tree.

Amanda felt a bit of anger. "It's quite rude to eavesdrop, and Charles is a wonderful man."

"Is that so?"

"Yes. He and Ma have treated me like family."

Luke continued carving into the tree as he spoke, but did so with less hostility. "Be careful, Amanda, I don't trust him."

"Why?"

"Just don't." Luke sheathed his knife. "Tell me about Louise."

"Why would you be interested in her?"

"Just am," he insisted. "What does she look like?"

Amanda sighed. "She is about my height, has brown hair and blue eyes, and I discovered today, after combing her hair, that she is very attractive. Are you interested in her personally? She's quite ill." Amanda couldn't resist getting back at him for eavesdropping. "But I'll introduce you as soon as she's feeling better." Luke didn't take her baiting. He looked disappointed. "What's wrong, Luke, not your type?"

"Tell me about her illness." His concern seemed sincere, so Amanda told him all she knew

He contemplated her story for several moments, then shook his head and said softly, "Please, Amanda, be careful of Pierce. He isn't what you think he is. Trust me, please."

Amanda noticed the sincerity in his eyes. "Luke, it's very thoughtful of you to worry, but I see no reason why Charles Pierce shouldn't be trusted or why I should be careful."

"He's had a lot of practice charming women. Please heed my warning. Be wary of Ma, too." He touched her cheek lightly and was gone.

After a hurried breakfast, Charles saddled a horse and rode toward the wagon trains ahead. He tossed Amanda a kiss as he trotted off. Amanda would have savored the sign of affection, except that Luke had appeared at that moment with an expression she couldn't remember ever seeing on Phillip's face. Was it anger? Fear? Worry? She wasn't sure, but knew he was upset

Luke mysteriously disappeared for two days. *Perhaps he is avoiding me,* Amanda thought, but later she overheard

Larsen complaining to Griff that he didn't know where Luke had gone.

The train moved on. It was high summer now, but the days became hot and the nights cool as they climbed to higher altitudes. One afternoon they had to stop the train because of a hailstorm with ice the size of snowballs.

During the layover a woman from four wagons behind sought out Amanda, knocking frantically on the wooden part of the wagon.

"Miss Barker!"

Amanda peeked out at the woman, huddled against the hail and wind, with just a shawl for protection.

"Goodness," she called above the noise of the storm. "Do come in!"

It was hard to guess the ages of the wagon-train women. The stress and rigors of this life made them look older Amanda classed this woman as somewhere in her thirties. Water dripped from her frizzily curled fair hair and pale, plain face.

"I'm Eliza Warner, and my baby is sick," she gasped all in one breath. "I'm scared it's that cholera. Would you come look at her?"

"Me?" Amanda was taken by surprise at the request.

"I heard your family died of it. Thought you'd recognize someone who had it. Would you?"

"I'm not sure." But Amanda grabbed her cape, and the women jumped from the wagon into the storm. As they walked backwards against the wind Amanda could feel the balls of ice pounding her body through the wool covering and wondered how painful it must feel through just a thin shawl. She spread out her cape and encircled the thin woman beside her. Eliza's smile thanked Amanda as they trudged toward the Warner wagon.

Amanda knew they'd reached the right wagon when she

heard the piercing screams of Eliza's baby. Once inside Amanda knelt beside the infant and felt the child's forehead. She asked Eliza questions about the baby's elimination and vomiting, then shook her head. "It's not cholera "

"Oh, thank You, Lord," Eliza whispered.

As the baby stiffened and let out another piercing holler, Amanda rubbed the baby's stomach soothingly

"What's your baby's name?"

"Suzannah "

"A pretty name for a pretty baby girl."

"Thank you. Do you know what's wrong with her?"

"I think Suzannah is cutting her first tooth."

"How do you know?" Eliza asked quickly

Amanda stood. "I helped Mama with Hazel Jane, my baby sister, and I remember every detail of her infant days They sometimes run a slight fever with cutting teeth; she's drooling a great deal; and look at her biting frantically at her fists. You said her diaper changes were normal, and she hasn't vomited. Her fever is so slight. It has to be a tooth Besides, she looks just about the right age to be cutting one. About four months?"

"Five," Eliza answered. "she was born in Saint Louis while we waited for the wagon train to start rolling."

Amanda looked about the wagon. "What can we do to make Suzannah more comfortable? Have you any camphor?"

"Yes, my mother packed a whole kit of medicines for us." She reached under the baby's cradle, pulled out a box, and handed it to Amanda. Amanda poured camphor on a small corner of a clean rag and rubbed the baby's reddened gums, then picked up Suzannah and rocked her gently to sleep.

"Thank you, Amanda," Eliza whispered when Suzannah was tucked back into her cradle. "My husband will want to thank you, too. Someone said there was a doctor on the train behind us, so he rode back to find him." She laughed. "How horribly embarrassed I'll be if he brings one back in this storm—for only a tooth!"

"We won't tell him then!" Amanda laughed back. "We'll let him make the diagnosis! But seriously, it can't hurt to have her looked at, just in case."

Eliza laughed again, and Amanda realized that without her worried look she wasn't as old as she'd thought, but closer to her own age.

"I have this urge to offer you tea, Amanda, but I've no fire to heat water! I can't get used to this rustic life." She laughed heartily. "Some hostess I am!"

Amanda laughed with her. How nice it was to have found a friend. They chatted until the hail and rain stopped, then Amanda said good-bye, promising to stop and visit often.

Approaching her wagon, she was surprised to see Luke leaning against it.

"Hi! Miss me?" He smiled.

"Oh, did you go somewhere?" she said as seriously as she could, which wasn't easy after just laughing and having fun with Eliza. She was in a teasing mood. Poor Luke, his face hung in disappointment at her words.

"You didn't notice? I was gone two days!'

"I hadn't seen you but didn't realize you weren't here at all. Where on earth would you go out here?"

"Scouting. This is Indian territory. Most are friendly, but my job is to make sure."

"If the Indians are friendly," Amanda challenged, "how is it people on the train are having things stolen?" *And,* she wondered, *if you were out scouting, why didn't Larsen know about it?*

"Like what?" he asked.

"Mr. Stegman slept under his wagon last night, and the

comforter was taken right off him as he slept. Then Mrs O'Day said her best bucket was taken from the hook at the side of her wagon. The lady in the wagon behind us is missing a pair of shoes! She'd taken them off to wash her feet, turned around, and they were gone!"

"Usually," Luke explained, "they try to barter for these things, but either the people wouldn't bargain, or the Indians here are too poor to trade. At least they aren't killing to get things. Thank God for that."

"I have nothing to thank God for," she snapped.

Luke started to say something but seemed to change his mind. Instead he took her hands and asked, "Will you do me a favor?"

"Since we're friends, I will try," she answered.

"It's a mighty big one. I need you to do something that may seem strange, without asking questions. I guess that's called trust. Do you trust me, Amanda?" he asked, squeezing her hand.

"Right now, I trust you more than anyone, but don't feel too flattered, my list of friends and family is extremely short these days."

"Amanda, don't be bitter. Remember, the weeds."
He touched her cheek with his hand tenderly.

She smiled. "That always gets to me, you know. Reminds me of Pa and Phillip." She pulled her hands from his. "All right, what's the favor?"

Luke suddenly took on a serious face, one foreign to Amanda. "Tomorrow night, after you feed Louise, can you get Helen to come to your wagon for ten or fifteen minutes?"

"Probably. But why—?" His hand snuffed out her words as it gently tapped her mouth.

"No questions. Trust me?"

"Yes. I'll try."

33

"Thank you. Good night," he said, kissing her cheek lightly.

Stunned by his action, she looked up at him in puzzlement.

"You could at least look dreamy for me," he said, pouting. "Like you did when Charles kissed your forehead."

"But," she explained as she climbed into her wagon, "I did that *after* he left." She closed the rear flap. "Good night, Luke."

4

*I*t hadn't rained since the day after Amanda buried her family. The trail was dry, hard, and dusty. There were several wagons delayed due to broken axles, springs, or wheels. Eliza walked with Amanda, carrying Suzannah in a tote upon her back, Indian style.

Charles had not returned, and Luke had waved briefly as he rode ahead early that morning with Griff.

Around noon, Luke and Griff kicked up a storm of dust, riding back to the train. They reined in their horses and spoke animatedly to Mr. Larsen, who called several men together before the train continued.

Luke rode back to where Amanda and Eliza walked. Amanda introduced Luke and Eliza. They continued to walk as Luke rode slowly beside Amanda. Anxious to hear his news, they gave him their complete attention.

"Ever see an Indian?" he asked.

"Not up close," answered Amanda.

"My husband, Martin, and I traded blankets for antelope

35

meat with an Indian a week ago. But I just looked on from a distance," said Eliza. "Why?"

Luke scooped his hair back and smiled boyishly. "We are about to go through a small Indian village."

"Is it safe?" both women cried at once.

"Quite. What do you think Griff and I do?"

Eliza and Amanda looked at each other and smiled.

"If you have anything to trade, this would be a good opportunity. But be careful, some of them are shrewd."

"Can you stay with us?" Amanda asked timidly.

"Sure." He grinned.

Soon the village came into sight. Amanda counted fifteen wigwams and guessed they had nearly a hundred ponies.

"Do they live right here in the open all the time?" Amanda asked.

"No, this is a temporary camp. They are probably here just for the summer, to trade with the wagon trains. Looks like they're ready to trade plenty of ponies."

While they lunched along the Platte banks, they watched another wagon train on the trail across the river. They were never out of sight of other wagon trains, and that Amanda thought most comforting.

Before they broke camp, their train was visited by an Indian chief who rode proudly up to Mr. Larsen on a mule whose bridle was covered with silver plates and emblems. The chief had a looking glass and comb suspended by a string and all sizes and shapes of ornamental coins and trinkets hanging from his garb. He wore silver earrings almost seven inches long. Amanda and Eliza stared at the sight and even remarked that, despite all his extravagance, he was a fine-looking man.

That evening the campers could barely prepare their dinners. Swarms of Indians hovered around, trying to swap moccasins and lariats for money, powder, and whiskey. Martin traded a bucket for a pair of moccasins for Eliza, and Larsen bought enough antelope meat for the whole train to buy and cook in shares.

After dinner, Amanda remembered her promise to Luke. She fed Louise, then asked Ma to help her move a trunk in her wagon. It was a good excuse, because the trunk really did need moving, and she'd mentioned it to Ma several times before.

Afterwards they chatted; then Ma said good night and left. Amanda had just finished preparing for bed and was just rolling back her blanket when Ma's frantic calling brought her to the rear flap.

"Ma! What's wrong?"

"It's Louise! She's gone! Did you feed her? Was she all right when you left her? Did she eat all her oatmeal with the medication?"

"Gone!" Amanda gasped. "She was sound asleep when I left her! How could she be gone?" Amanda grabbed her heavy cape, swung it around her, and hurried after Ma toward the other wagon. She answered Ma's questions on the way. "Of course I fed her. She ate every bit. Are you sure she didn't slip off her bedroll or something?"

They climbed into the wagon, and Ma lit a candle.

Louise *was* missing.

Amanda tossed restlessly upon her bedroll, too many unanswered questions rattling through her brain. Why had Luke wanted Ma away from Louise? What had Luke to do with Louise and her disappearance? Why hadn't Ma wanted the incident reported to Larsen? Perhaps the men could have organized a search party for poor Louise. Instead, Ma had just said to wait for Charles's return. It didn't make sense.

One thing she knew for sure: She trusted Luke enough

not to mention his part in Louise's disappearance—at least not yet. Had it been merely a coincidence? Had Luke another reason to want Ma away from her wagon? Why would Luke kidnap Louise? If he had, where would he have hidden her? Could Indians have taken Louise? She had plenty of questions for Luke.

Ma was quiet at breakfast, which Amanda thought odd, as most mothers would be frantic instead of silent and moody.

"Aren't you going to have Larsen and the men look for Louise?" Amanda finally asked.

"I don't know what to do," she said. "I wish Charles would come back. Yet when he does, he'll be madder than . . . ." She broke off.

"Do you think those Indians took her?" Amanda asked.

"Charles'll handle this. I don't trust anyone else." Ma scratched her head in confusion. "It had to be the Indians, who else would take her? Who else?" she repeated.

Just before the wagons were positioned to roll, Amanda spotted Luke washing his dishes in the river. She ran to join him, greeting him warmly.

"Got a present for you," he said, reaching into his breast pocket.

"You have?" She looked down at his outstretched hand. "It's lovely," she exclaimed reaching for the string of brightly colored Indian beads.

"Did you barter with the Indians, too?"

"A little."

"Thank you, they're lovely." She swung them over her head and patted them into place gently. "How do they look?"

For once Luke's face was serious. He put his thumb under her chin and raised her head. "Perfect."

Breaking the spell of his eyes and gentleness, Amanda moved away and asked, "What have you done with Louise?"

"What makes you think I did anything with Louise?"

"She's missing."

"I thought that was your job, watching her? Fine job you did, if she's missing," he said blandly.

"You!" she nearly choked. "You told me to—"

"Sh-h-h," he warned. "Keep your voice down. That's our secret, remember?"

"But I didn't know you'd use me to . . . to . . . do something dishonest!"

"Trust me."

"Why?"

"Because I'm your friend." He kissed her hand and hurried away, leaving her with unanswered questions and frustrated feelings.

Careful not to mention the incident with Louise to her new friend, Amanda scuffed alongside her wagon with Eliza and the baby. Yet this new mystery kept her silent and contemplative. She had the feeling Eliza was about to ask about her preoccupation when a cloud of dust approaching the train caught their attention. Amanda thought it might be Luke again, but it was Charles. He saw Amanda, took off his hat, and waved before tethering his horse to the back of his wagon and hopping up alongside Ma, who drove Amanda's wagon.

Ma was right, Amanda noticed at lunchtime; Charles *was* angry. While they ate, he paced back and forth, banging his fist into the back of the wagon once or twice. Several times he stopped and scanned the campers carefully, as if looking for a certain person, then continued his pacing with an angry, puzzled expression.

Finally, after cleaning up after lunch, Amanda found the courage to approach Charles. "Aren't you going to hunt for her?" She spoke while his back was turned, and he spun around in surprise at her voice.

"Of course. You didn't think I'd just let those savages have her, did you?" She was glad he didn't sound angry.

"Does this mean you'll no longer need me?" she asked timidly.

"Of course not!" He took her hand and rubbed it gently, giving her goose bumps. "You're family—no matter what, you are staying with us."

"Will you leave soon to search for her?"

"Immediately. I just wish. . . ."

She tilted her head, wondering what he wished.

"I wish I didn't have to leave again. I just got back. I missed you," he whispered, squeezing her small hand.

"Missed me?" Her heart thundered beneath her ribs.

He dropped her hand, "But now I have something pleasant to look forward to when I return." He untied his horse, mounted, and rode westward with a wave of his hat.

"How sweet!"

Amanda jumped and spun around. "Luke!" she gasped. Tapping her foot impatiently, she added, "You have to stop spying on me like that. Can't I have any privacy?"

"Not when you select friends so carelessly."

"Carelessly? What's wrong with Charles? And why is it your concern?"

"Charles is a . . . a . . .," he seemed too angry to grasp the right word. "And it *is* my concern, if we're friends. Isn't it?" he added, looking like Phillip again.

Amanda immediately softened. Luke didn't arouse the exciting thrill in her that Charles did, but he had a way with her that she couldn't explain.

"Of course, it is. I'm sorry." She smiled. "It's just that I like Charles. He's been good to me. Give him a chance. If it weren't for him. . . . " She hesitated.

"Just be careful," he warned again. "If you want to be friendly to him, fine, but promise me one thing: Don't trust him. Okay?"

Amanda studied Luke carefully. His personality confused her. He reflected Phillip's boyish innocence one moment and was serious, mature, and intelligent the next. Of one thing she was almost certain: His concern for her was sincere. "I promise."

Charles returned two days later without Louise but with another rider whom Amanda immediately distrusted. Arabella—or Bella, as they introduced her—was young, fair, blue eyed, and wore too much powder and lipstick. Holding her head high, she seemed arrogant and distant, yet Amanda noticed she hung on Charles's every word and looked at him adoringly.

Charles explained that while he had no luck finding Louise, Bella had asked to transfer to this train from the one ahead. She claimed she couldn't get along with one of the girls in her wagon.

"Who is this Bella?" Amanda asked Ma later.

"Charles didn't tell you?"

Amanda laughed. "If he had, I wouldn't be asking you!"

"Oh, sure." She chuckled. "She's just one of the girls. You know, who will work for us in Frisco."

"A friend?"

"Well," Ma hesitated. "Not exactly. We met her in Saint Louis. She needed a job and wanted to go west . . ., so we offered to bring her with us. As Charles said, we have five wagons going out with numerous new workers."

"She seems to adore Charles."

"They all do." Ma chuckled. Then seeing Amanda's disappointment, she added, "But you're special."

"Why do you say that?"

"Because I know Charles. These girls will all be working for him, so he has to be nice to them. You aren't one of his workers. He chose you to travel with us because you're special. There's a difference. Believe me, I can tell."

Amanda smiled and returned to her wagon. Before falling asleep, she chuckled to herself over her predicament. Here she was out in the middle of nowhere, in the company of a strange couple, friends with a man who had made her an accomplice in a mysterious predicament, and attracted to two men in completely different ways.

She sobered suddenly and thought about the recent deaths. At least with everything else happening she hadn't had time to dwell on her family. She also missed her nightly prayers, yet still couldn't bring herself to talk to God. Not after what He had allowed to happen. She missed the comfort of prayer but had simply lost faith in it and Him.

Then she heard someone knocking on the wood of her wagon from the rear.

She sat up in bed, listening carefully.

"Amanda," a male voice whispered.

Amanda crawled to the rear flap and stuck her head out. "Luke!" she whispered in surprise.

"Can you come out a minute?"

"You're a little late. I'm in bed already."

"Please?"

"Wait," she said, "I'll throw on my cape."

Hastily she donned her cape and jumped out the back of the wagon. Luke walked her a small distance from the wagons before questioning her.

"Who is the new girl with Charles?"

"Bella."

"Where'd she come from?" he asked in astonishment.

"One of his other wagons on another train."

"How many wagons does he have?"

"Five."

"This girl, what's she like?" At Amanda's puzzled look he added, "I mean is she happy to be here? She isn't ill like Louise or anything?"

"No, she's quite well and quite happy to be anywhere near Charles."

Luke fondled his chin and mumbled to himself.

"Is something wrong?"

"I'm not sure."

"What's going on?" she asked. "And where is Louise? I know you had something to do with her disappearance."

He changed the subject quickly. "Helen isn't Charles's mother, is she?"

"No. They just wanted to appear as a family unit. She's his business partner in a hotel. The girls, I believe, are to be workers there. Bella is one of them. They found her in Saint Louis."

"What type of work did they tell you the girls would be doing?"

"Hostesses' work, maids, singers, dancers—"

"Charles told you that?"

"Yes."

"I see. Yet you seem fond of this man and even sounded jealous of Bella. How could you be attracted to a man involved in this type of business?"

"This type of business?" she repeated. "His hotel happens to be an elegant establishment, the best this side of the Mississippi."

Luke looked at her sadly and shook his head. "Perhaps you should find out more about this man you seem so taken with."

Confused by Luke's questions, Amanda said a quick good night and hurried back to her wagon and bedroll.

5

When camping grounds were agreeable and the wagon train not in danger, they did not travel on Sunday The men mended wagons, harnesses, and yokes, shod animals, and did other general maintenance. The women washed clothes; boiled beans in large quantities, to be warmed during the week; or mended and cleaned.

A devotional service was held in the morning. Old Mr Simpson, a Methodist church elder for thirty years, stood in the center of the corral and read from the Bible and preached while most kept on with their work. No disrespect was intended, for there was little time for leisure.

Luke had stopped by and invited Amanda to the service but she had declined in favor of washing clothes. As she hung her laundry on a rope stretched between her wagon and the Pierces she could hear most of the devotional anyway. She noticed only a handful actually sat and listened; most were legitimately too busy.

Charles and his driver, Albert, were patching a hole in the

tent in which they slept. Bella was helping Ma arrange the Pierces' wagon to accommodate Bella's things and still have enough room for them to sleep comfortably. Amanda could hear them arguing over the lack of space and whose things should go where.

Deciding to help Ma with the difficult situation, Amanda walked over to the wagon. "I have a little extra room in my wagon, if you'd like to store some things, Ma," she offered.

"Take this female off my hands, that's what you can do!" Ma yelled back.

"I wouldn't share a wagon with that plain farm girl," Bella snapped. "*You* share her wagon!"

"Plain farm girl! Amanda's got more class in her baby finger than you'll ever have in your whole body! And she's a lady, too! Now take that trunk and put it on your side of the wagon!" Ma ordered.

"Now hold it . . . ," Bella started to say between her teeth.

"What's going on?" Charles bellowed from behind Amanda, causing her to jump.

Both Ma and Bella gave their accounts of the problem at the same time, causing Charles to hold his hands over his ears.

"Quiet! Both of you be still this instant!" Charles motioned to Ma. "Come here a moment."

They talked in low tones, with Charles continually having to hush Ma, when her voice got louder as she became excited, telling her side of the story.

Finally he turned to Amanda, who stood nearby, and motioned to her. "Amanda, come here a second, please. Ma says you have space in your wagon. Would you be kind enough to store a few things for us?"

"Certainly," she said.

Charles walked over to the pouting Bella and talked to her in soft tones until she smiled adoringly at him.

Later, while Charles lifted the trunk into her wagon, Amanda said, "You handled that situation very diplomatically. I couldn't help but admire your skill at dealing with the dilemma."

"I get plenty of practice at the hotel. My women—the workers—are always squabbling." He turned, sat on the trunk, and sighed. "Some men think I'm lucky working with lovely women, but let me tell you, if it's not fighting, it's one female problem after another. Which is probably why I stayed single so long," he said with a smile and wink. But his usual sparkle was missing.

"You don't look your usual self today. Are you well?" she asked.

"I'm fine. I just didn't sleep well last night."

"No? I'm sorry to hear that. That's one thing I don't hear complaints on very often; most everyone is exhausted come nightfall on the trail," Amanda said.

"I usually am too, but . . . well," he faltered. "Something—or should I say someone—woke me, and then I was too upset to sleep."

Amanda tilted her head, trying to comprehend his problem.

"Actually," he explained, "it has to do with you, my dear."

"Me?" she whispered, more puzzled than ever.

"Yes. I've become quite fond of you, as you probably have guessed and was quite upset when your late-night visitor woke me. Then I saw the two of you walk toward those bushes," he pointed, "and whisper for some time. Besides a touch of jealousy, I'm concerned for your welfare. Just who is this fellow?"

"That was just my friend Luke West. He's a hired hand for the train."

Charles rubbed his forehead as if trying to remember something. "Luke West. No, never heard of him."

"Is that so strange? I've never heard of anyone else on this train either."

Charles hesitated as if lost for words, then answered, "Yes, you're right, it's just that he looked familiar." Charles straightened. "Well, time to get back to my tent mending."

"What about Louise?" Amanda asked before he could climb out of her wagon.

"Haven't a clue as to where she is or who took her. I've got people from the other trains working on it. We suspect those Indians. Some of the more primitive tribes still use white women for slaves and even sell them."

Amanda paled. "They do?"

"Certainly. Now that we're traveling into more dangerous Indian country, I'd not wander far from the others. Otherwise you have little to fear." He jumped from the wagon. "Thank you for letting us use some of your wagon space." He winked. "See you at supper."

As Amanda folded her dry laundry she wondered at Bella's words: *plain farm girl.* Why did the girl dislike her? Not that Amanda was fond of Bella either, but she wondered why the girl continued to shun her and give her unkind looks.

Amanda wondered if Bella was in love with Charles. Did Bella suspect Charles's interest in her? That would certainly explain the hatred toward her.

Could I fall in love with a man such as Charles Pierce? He is handsome, charming, rich . . . . Any girl would be lucky to have him interested in her, yet . . . . Amanda's thoughts faltered, and Luke's face popped into her head. *What about Luke? One* man gave her goose bumps, the other a warm feeling in her chest. Luke was a good, respectable, God-fearing man. While Charles's reputation was questionable, it seemed to make him more exciting. Amanda had never known a man such as Charles.

Ma and Amanda prepared supper while Bella sat by the river, combing her hair and powdering her nose. Ma grumbled about Bella's laziness, and Amanda soothed her anger by reminding Ma that Bella's not helping was probably a blessing in disguise.

"You're right!" Ma laughed. "She'd make a mess of everything!"

Charles sat beside Amanda during supper. Bella sat behind the wagon, giving Amanda looks of pure hatred. Afterwards Charles invited Amanda to walk around the circle of wagons with him. He told her about San Francisco, which he called Frisco, and the hotel.

As he talked about the large, strange city Amanda began to worry. How would she find Aunt Hattie? What if Aunt Hattie had died, too? Where would she go? What would she do?

When they returned to Amanda's wagon, she looked up at him in the moonlight and asked, "What if things go wrong for me when I reach San Francisco? What if I'm left alone in that big city?"

Charles stood silently, apparently taken completely by surprise. Amanda explained. "I'm supposed to find my father's sister, Aunt Hattie, but I worry about finding her. What would I do alone in a big, strange city?"

Charles laughed, taking her hand in his. "Amanda, as long as I'm in the same city, you have nothing to fear. I'd not let anything happen to you." He sobered somewhat before adding, "There's always my hotel. You'd be my guest for as long as need be."

"Oh, I'd have to earn my keep," she said firmly.

"If it ever comes to that, we'll arrange something we can both agree to," he said, leaning over to kiss her forehead. "Good night, my lovely Amanda."

After he'd left, Amanda peered about cautiously, half expecting Luke to pop out of the brush with a sarcastic remark. When he didn't, she felt disappointed yet wondered why, when Charles had been so charming.

She climbed into her wagon and felt in the darkness for her kerosene lamp. The light flickered and finally caught, and Amanda jumped as she caught a shadow on her bedroll. She was not alone. Holding the lamp out toward the figure, she could see the face of her visitor.

"What are you doing here, Bella?"

"I came to give you some advice," she spat from reddened lips. The lamp's reflection on her eyes made her look sinister.

"What kind of advice would you have for me?" Amanda asked with a touch of sarcasm.

"Charles is not your type. Stay away from him."

"Because *you* want him?"

"Because he's not what you think he is. I heard you talking. What kind of hotel do you think he and Ma run? There's gambling, drinking, dancing, and—"

"I think you had better leave, Bella."

Bella edged toward the back opening. "Charles wants you, but not for the reasons you think. He has customers who will pay big money for—"

"*Bella!*"

Amanda recognized Ma's shrill voice from outside the wagon. Ma's head popped through the rear flap. "Bella, get back to the wagon! Charles is furious! We aren't supposed to be out wandering alone." In a calmer voice, Ma continued, "We were quite worried about you."

It seemed to Amanda that after that evening Ma and Charles did everything they could to keep Bella and her apart. Were they afraid of what Bella had been trying to tell about Charles, or were they merely trying to keep peace? Bella had said Charles had customers who would pay big money for. . . . For what? What did this have to do with her?

Yet Amanda had little time to wonder, for Luke had disappeared again. This time Larsen came to Amanda's wagon, looking for him.

"Isn't he scouting for you?" she asked.

"No, and Griff is throwing a tantrum over it. Ve are beginning to travel into hostile Indian territory. Not only that, but ve need help vith the animals. He just disappears for days! Vere could he go?" Larsen scratched his head. "I thought maybe he vas helping you again."

"I'm sorry, Mr. Larsen, I have no idea where he is," she apologized as the poor, bewildered man walked back toward the corral.

Where, Amanda wondered, *could Luke disappear to out in this God-forsaken wilderness?*

Two days later, Luke reappeared. He tipped his hat to Amanda from a distance but never approached her.

Amanda had little time to worry about whether or not Luke was in trouble or wonder why he didn't stop by. The day before, they had arrived at Fort Laramie, where they had stopped to camp and pick up supplies. It was their last civilized post before reaching Fort Bridger. Ma and Amanda packed and repacked their supplies to best fit their cramped quarters.

The day Luke returned, the train had had a difficult river crossing, in high, swift water. Luckily the river hadn't been deep enough to warrant taking the wheels off the wagons and floating them across, as they'd done a few weeks ago. Yet the wagons became wet and muddy—inside and out. Ma and Amanda worked hard at keeping their wagons clean and comfortable. Bella managed to look busy whenever Charles looked her way, but she shirked her responsibility most of the time.

Charles tried to spend time with Amanda during the few minutes of free time the travelers enjoyed between cleaning up after the evening meal and going to bed. On less hectic days, campfires were lit and campers sang and told stories.

Tonight, with the crossing behind them, the cleanup completed, and loaded with new supplies and good spirits, the campers made a bonfire and celebrated.

Charles, Amanda, Eliza, and Martin listened intently as Jeb Colter wove the best campfire tale Amanda had ever heard. All four believed his account of a confrontation with hostile Indians, until the punch-line ending, which had them laughing and shivering at the same time.

Charles's hand covered Amanda's beneath her apron, which was spread upon the ground. She looked up at him and for the first time didn't feel goose bumps, but a lump in her throat. Between Luke's warnings and Bella's advice, Amanda no longer felt sure she wanted Charles's advances. Perhaps he wasn't her type of man.

Flames leapt from his eyes, reflecting the bonfire. He looked like Satan at that moment, smiling down at her with fiery eyes.

Is that what I've come to? she wondered. *I've given up God in my life, but that doesn't mean I have to let my life slide over to Satan. Does it? Is that what Charles, Ma, Bella, and the hotel are in my life?* Amanda shivered.

Charles put his jacket over her shoulders, his hands lingering too long.

How silly, she thought, shaking off the evil premonition. Just because Bella, Charles and Ma used a little cussing and ran a hotel that had gambling, dancing, drinking, and fun didn't mean they were straight from hades. Yet the ill feeling stayed with her.

The yawning group finally broke up, and Charles walked Amanda back to her wagon, still holding her hand.

"You seem distant tonight," he said. "Is something the matter?"

Amanda hesitated. He asked so sincerely and with such charm, her first instinct was to tell him her true thoughts—Satan, fiery eyes, and all! She stopped herself. She'd promised Luke not to trust him.

"I'm extremely tired is all."

"You've been a bit distant since the night Bella visited your wagon." He stopped walking and, placing his hands on her shoulders, turned her toward him. "Did she say something to upset you?"

Amanda hesitated again. It was difficult to lie when a man had you looking straight into his eyes—and such handsome eyes!

"I-I . . . ," she faltered.

"She's jealous is all," he laughed lightly. "She, as well as anyone, can see where my interest lies."

"Your interest lies?" Amanda repeated for lack of another response.

"With you, Amanda," he whispered, gripping her shoulders more tightly.

"Why me?" she asked, no longer excited by his touch but frightened by it.

He shook his head, smiling. "I've never met a girl like you. You're beautiful, refined, intelligent, kind, yet so pure and innocent." He moved his hands from her shoulders to her face. Caressing her cheeks, he whispered, "I hadn't meant to ask this yet, but will you marry me when we get to Frisco?"

Amanda found it difficult to think with him stroking her cheeks and murmuring sweet words. She stepped back, causing his hands to fall from her face.

"I need to think . . . ," she said.

He threw up his hands. "You mean without me crowding you?"

She nodded.

'I understand, but let me just give you a few things to consider. I'm a very wealthy man. I not only own one of the largest hotels in San Francisco, but a mansion on a hill overlooking the bay. You would live as a princess, with servants to wait upon your every need. Anything your heart desired would be yours, just by asking.'

"What kind of life would we lead?" she asked. "I mean there are other things more important to me. For instance how do you feel about a family? Would you be a faithful loving husband? How would your hotel affect our lives? Do you attend a church?'

Charles whispered a mild oath and threw back his head laughing. "When you said you needed time to think, I thought you'd need a day or two! Such deep, serious questions to come up just moments after my proposal. How your mind works!'

"But I've been considering along these lines for several days now, in case this sort of thing did happen. In fact, I've been quite worried about the difference in our backgrounds

"All right, he said calmly "Let me answer your questions then. I'd love to have at least half a dozen children and with you as my wife I'd be the most faithful and loving husband. My business would be business and my personal life my personal life. Finally, I've never been to church and never planned on making it a part of my life. However, if it were important to you, I would seriously consider at least trying it." He shrugged, "Does that give you enough to give me an answer?"

She smiled. He could be so charming and accommodating. "I'll give you my answer tomorrow night. Is that fair enough?"

"More than fair." He kissed her lips gently before heading quickly toward his tent.

Confused by her lack of enthusiasm, Amanda even shocked herself by rubbing the wetness of his kiss from her lips.

Why had her feelings for him changed so suddenly? Was it Bella's warning? Luke? Or the premonition of evil his fiery eyes had put into her mind that evening? She shivered and climbed into her wagon.

6

Due to the wagon train's strenuous and demanding life, slumber seldom became a problem even under these primitive conditions. Amanda contemplated her love life and decisions for just the briefest time before falling deeply asleep. Sleeping soundly, she did not awaken when several figures climbed into the rear of her wagon. Not until the crouched shadows touched her as she slept did she start in fright.

Gasping, she held her blanket to her throat and strained to see in the darkness. The intruders stood frozen over her bedroll. When her eyes adjusted and focused, she could make out four men. She recognized them as Indians by their colorful dress, headbands, and painted faces. The whites of their eyes glowed ominously in the darkness.

Too numb to speak, Amanda froze in the corner of her bedroll, blanket pulled tightly to her chin. She wondered if this were a dream and she'd awaken any second and laugh over this nightmare. Then the tallest Indian nudged the short, stocky one beside him and she knew this was real.

The short Indian covered her mouth while the tall one reached for her arms. Though gentle, the men were firm. Amanda panicked and kicked and fought—to no avail.

Competently, they tied her hands, bound something clothlike about her mouth, and tied it behind her head. The third Indian roped her feet together while the fourth wrapped her tightly inside her own blanket.

She lay completely helpless as they lifted and threw her gently over the tall Indian's shoulder. They had done it all in complete silence. Out of habit, Amanda began to pray, then caught herself quickly: *I can't pray! He didn't help me before, why should He now?*

Feeling the cool air on her face and the gait of the man beneath her, Amanda knew they were not only out into the night, but running at a swift pace. Often she felt tree limbs snap her face or snag her blanket. She recalled seeing woods near their camp and knew she was now being carried through them.

Stories she'd heard about what Indians did to white women raced through her mind. Amanda recalled seeing women recoil from the terrible tales and hearing them tell how they would kill themselves before letting an Indian molest them.

Amanda had stopped fighting once they'd tied her securely. It would be useless and waste her strength. She relaxed now as she was toted through the darkness.

They seemed to travel for hours. Their pace, which had slowed from a run to a trot, now became a fast walk, which suited her better, as it jostled her less.

A stray thought darted through Amanda's mind: *They've been so gentle—at least so far!* They hadn't spoken either, she realized. Had they treated her roughly and spoken to her rudely, she'd have been frantic, instead of merely frightened. Where were they taking her and why?

Finally Amanda could see the light of dawn filtering through the foliage. *Whatever the ordeal, it has to be better to face it in daylight,* she thought with relief.

Moments later her entourage came to a sudden halt. Where were they? The tall Indian eased her from his shoulder and set her down, while another took her by the shoulders and slid her sideways into a tent. As she quickly glanced at the stranger who'd carried her, another kind of fear overwhelmed Amanda. *He was not an Indian.*

Fear clutched at her throat. *Why would a white man disguise himself as an Indian?* It seemed more forboding than a bona fide Indian. Did these men have foul play in mind? Who were they, and why did they want her?

Closing the tent flap behind them, they left her alone, lying upon her back. Their shadows leapt against the outside of the tent, and whispers broke the silence.

She struggled with her bonds, but they remained secure as she knew they would. Amanda could do nothing but wait. Suddenly the reality of the situation hit her like a hammer. Her fright, her helplessness, and even sudden thoughts of home and Mama, Pa, Phillip, and Hazel Jane flooded her mind. All self-control and bravery gone, she began to cry softly, then loudly, until her weeping became full-fledged sobs of despair.

She hadn't wanted to crumble, but though she tried to stop, she couldn't. The sobs grew louder. Through her tears she noticed the tent become flooded with light as someone opened the flap and entered. Amanda had no idea what effect her sobbing would have on her captors. Would they become angry? Would they kill her? For all her fears and trying, she could not cease.

The man who'd entered the tent touched her shoulder

gently. "Please don't cry," he whispered sympathetically.

Surprised by the tenderness, Amanda's tears subsided somewhat. Reduced to those horrid after-crying hiccups, she stared blankly at the man. It was the tall one, who'd carried her. He still had the white stripes painted on his cheeks but seemed less terrifying.

"There, there." He patted her head. "No one is going to harm you. I promise. We didn't hurt you, did we?" He gently removed the cloth binding her mouth.

Amanda stared at him. Despite his war paint and the bandana with a feather and all, he looked not only friendly but familiar. Yet she knew she'd never met this man before.

"W-who are y-you?" she stuttered between hiccups.

"I can't tell you yet."

"W-why did you ta-take me?"

"For your own good, I can tell you that."

She looked at him curiously.

"When Luke gets here, he'll explain. He made us promise not to tell you a thing until he got here. But I couldn't bear hearing you cry." He looked down at her with soft gray eyes. "I have sisters . . . , and you seemed so distraught."

Amanda's eyes had widened the moment she'd heard Luke's name.

"L-Luke?" she stammered. "Luke who?"

The man smiled. "Luke Sterling, my brother."

"Oh! For a moment I thought you meant a friend of mine, Luke West."

He smiled. "Just relax and don't cry. We aren't going to harm you. Luke will explain everything as soon as he gets here."

He left the tent, and Amanda sighed with relief. Despite all her unanswered questions and fears, she fell soundly asleep.

The sound of male voices raised in greetings awoke

Amanda with a jolt. She mentally scolded herself for falling asleep at such a time. Here her life was in danger, and she slept. Had that young man's kindness relaxed her that much?

By the sound of things outside, their man Luke had arrived. Maybe now she'd find out what was going on. But when the figure burst into the tent, Amanda gasped in surprise and anger. "Luke West!"

He fell to his knees beside her. "Are you all right, Amanda?" he asked solicitously.

"You!" she cried. "What have you to do with this?"

"Answer me, first. Are you all right?" he insisted.

"Oh, I'm fine. I was kidnapped by four 'Indians,' toted piggyback through the forest, dumped into a tent, and left for who knows what purpose. My hands are tied behind me and numb; my feet are . . . ," she sighed.

"I've never been better," she continued sarcastically. "How kind of you to ask."

"Jared!" he yelled, without taking his eyes from hers. The tall, sympathetic man entered.

"Why is she still tied? Cut her free at once!"

"But you said—"

"Free her—at once!" Luke demanded.

Jared unsheathed the knife secured on his belt and rolled Amanda onto her side to slice through her ropes.

"You may leave," Luke ordered.

Jared shrugged and left the tent.

"Luke West," Amanda said between gritted teeth, "what is the meaning of this?"

"I'm not Luke West. I used that name on the train. My name is Luke Sterling."

Amanda closed her eyes. She was losing patience. "All right, Mr. Sterling, what is going on?"

"Three of those 'Indians' are my brothers, Jared, Aaron,

and Robert. The short one is a family friend and an actual half-breed Indian, whose name is Jonathan, but we all call him Jack. We come from a large ranch in Texas and are hunting for our sister Celia, whom we have been led to believe was coerced away by your fiancé, Mr. Pierce, in Saint Louis."

Amanda sighed. "First of all, Charles is not my fiancé. I doubt he coerced anyone. And you said your sister had died."

"I said I'd *lost* a loved one. We don't know if she is alive or not. We traced her to having been last seen with him. We've followed him, and we think we have him red-handed, stealing women for his . . . his *hotel* in San Francisco."

"Why do you say *hotel* in such a way? It *is* a hotel."

Luke looked away. "He runs a hotel that is also a gambling hall and brothel."

"Brothel!" Amanda gasped, blushing. "You mean, he— the women. . . ," She thought a moment, during the embarrassed silence, then asked, "How do you know all this?"

"We had him thoroughly investigated. While I traveled with the train, I kept my eye on him. From time to time I met my brothers at certain prearranged points, to get more information and to prepare to close in on him."

"So why kidnap *me?* Why didn't you grab *him?*"

"You were going to marry the . . . the—"

"I was not!"

"I heard the whole blasted conversation . . . ."

Amanda sat up, placed her hands on her hips, and cried, *"You listened?"*

Staring fixedly at the ground, Luke muttered, "Said I was keeping my eye on him."

Amanda sighed, shaking her head. "So you whisked me off so I wouldn't marry him? Is that it?"

"Partly. I also was protecting you from two other things."

"I can't wait to hear this," she said, rolling her eyes.

"He planned on using you in his establishment and had no intention of marrying you. While I was eavesdropping on you and him, I also spotted your friend Bella spying on you and Charles. She, I'm afraid, had something more sinister planned for you."

"How could you possibly know that Charles didn't really want to marry me?" she pouted.

"Because he used that same story on other girls. There are crazed people in this world, and right now most of them are out west, looking for gold. They actually pay money to be with innocent, sweet girls like yourself. The other kind of girls are a dime a dozen out there "

Amanda blushed. She knew he spoke the truth. Suddenly she recalled Louise "What about Louise? Did you steal her, too?" Amanda asked.

"Yep. She's on her way to our ranch now. My mother will help her get on her feet and find her family. Edward, my oldest brother, and Juan, one of our hands, are escorting her. As soon as the effect of Ma's medicine wore off, she was fine and gave me more information than anyone yet about your Charles."

· "That wasn't tonic in her oatmeal? Ma was drugging Louise?"

Luke nodded. "Under Charles's orders, and her name isn't Louise, but Frances Porter. She is from a farming family near Saint Louis, where she was coerced into friendship with Charles, then kidnapped and drugged. What do you think of wonderful Charles Pierce now?"

· Amanda crossed her arms. "I'm still mighty angry, Luke Sterling. Seems to me there could have been a less frightening way to do this. Couldn't you have warned me? Confided in me? This kidnapping was outrageous."

"I didn't have time. When I heard him propose and saw your dreamy look again, I gave the guys the signal. It had to be last night." He looked at her earnestly. "You wouldn't have believed me anyway. You thought him wonderful."

Amanda rubbed her temples. Too much had happened too fast. She could hardly believe Charles ran a brothel, though she knew it was true. All the pieces fit together. She wondered what effect all this would have on her and her plans to reach San Francisco and Aunt Hattie.

She studied him thoughtfully. "What will you do with me now?"

"I don't know. Have someone escort you back to the ranch, too, I suppose.'

She'd oppose that, she thought, yet said only "And you?"

"I'll continue to follow Pierce until he leads me to Celia or I discover what happened to her. I think Ma knows. Maybe I can get her to talk."

Hoping to try a different strategy on Luke, she offered, "It's possible I could be of help."

"No, from here on it becomes too dangerous."

Amanda's lower lip protruded in a childish pout. "I'm not going to any ranch. Either I help you find Celia, or I go back to the train." Then something occurred to her. She hit her head with her hand, "Oh, Luke, everything I own is in that wagon, *I have to go back!*"

"No." He stood and turned to leave the tent. "And if you argue, I'll have Jared tie you up again."

"You wouldn't!"

"Try me." He turned and left her alone with her anger.

Amanda pounded her fists into the side of the tent. *He*

can't do this to me! I've got to go back. I've got to get to San Francisco and dear Aunt Hattie.

Once washed clean in a small spring-fed creek, Amanda felt better but wished she had a decent dress. Mama had warned her to sleep in an old dress while on the trail, in case an emergency arose. That advice had been sound, yet Amanda felt uncomfortable in the loose, waistless, wrinkled cotton dress. She also pined for her other priceless possessions. How could she persuade Luke to let her return to the wagon train?

The smell of fried fish floated through the air, and her stomach nudged her, reminding her she hadn't eaten in some time. She followed the aroma to the nearby campfire. Sitting on a nearby stump, she studied the mysterious group of men around it.

Her eyes fell on Jared first—the tall one—taller than his brother Luke, yet as rugged, except his eyes weren't as expressive or sensitive. He was as pleasing to look upon as Luke, but lacked his brother's boyish charm. His best features, she decided, were his soft, kind face and compassionate nature.

Next she scanned the man Jared addressed as Aaron. While the others talked and joked as they cleaned, sliced, and fried fresh fish in a large frying pan over the open fire, he remained silent and contemplative. Perhaps he was a thinker. Not unsociable, merely separated by his private thoughts, he smiled now and then at some joke or statement but, Amanda thought, remained detached and in his own world.

His hair was black, unlike Luke or Jared's sandy heads. But he looked handsome, and appeared to prefer the indoors—perhaps reading.

A man they called Robert did most of the joking and

talking. His sense of humor seemed to keep everyone in a lively mood. His reddish-brown hair—his best feature—was thick and wavy. While also quite good looking, the large space between his front teeth created a whistle when he pronounced s sounds.

Amanda's eyes fell on a man who must be Jack, the half-breed. She chuckled to herself. Jared had looked more like an Indian last night than the real one did now. The only traits she could see in Jack that betrayed his heritage were his high cheekbones, straight but short black hair, and perhaps his small, dark eyes. His skin was only slightly darker than that of the other men. Jack's English was flawless. The other men were trying, without luck, to strip the fish of its spine and bones with one slice, as Jack could.

Looking up suddenly, Luke smiled, walked to where she sat, and said with all his boyish charm, "Still angry with me?"

Amanda spun around, showing him her back. She knew if she had looked at him a moment longer she'd have melted. No. If she was to get her way, she must not let him get the best of her.

She heard his arms fall to his sides and a sigh of frustration. Silence. Why didn't he speak? Was he plotting how to charm her into his good graces again? *Be strong,* she warned herself. *There is a lot at stake.* She must gain possession of her family's treasures, her clothes, and her wagon.

When the silence finally became too unbearable, she turned ever so slightly and peeked behind her. No wonder it was silent. He was gone. She spun the rest of the way around. The other men still bent over the fire, but Luke was missing. She stamped her foot. Now what was she to do?

7

"*A*manda!" Jared called. 'Come, have some fish. You must be hungry!"

Amanda sat beside Jared and took the offered fish. It was not, crispy, and tasty.

Robert introduced himself and handed her a tin cup of coffee. "Mom says it was my coffee that put hair on our chests— ' At her startled look and blush, he laughed. "But it only works for men—"

She smiled and took a sip.

'Except Aunt Hortense. ' Robert laughed.

Amanda nearly choked on her coffee.

'Quit teasing her," Jared scolded. "After last night we we her a little kindness and sympathy."

'I'm sorry, Amanda," Robert said earnestly. "My mouth works faster than my brain most of the time. I meant no harm. Sometimes humor makes tense situations lighter. I like to use humor to make those around me happy and forget their problems. Sometimes that works both ways and I do it to forget my own." His laugh was infectious and Amanda smiled.

"I think," the quiet man spoke for the first time, "you merely thrive on the attention your humor brings."

"Of course I do, Aaron, and who wouldn't want Amanda's attention?"

"More fish, Amanda?" Jack held out another piece.

She took it and smiled. "Thank you, you're all being kind. *Almost* all of you," she added in a whisper.

"Almost?" Jared poked Robert with his elbow. "See, you *have* offended her."

"No, Robert is charming," Amanda said. "All four of you are."

"Looks like Luke's the guilty one," Jared said. "Are you still upset over the kidnapping?"

"Yes. How did he think I'd feel? Now, when I want to return to the wagon train, he won't let me." Amanda noticed she had not only gotten their complete attention, but their sympathy as well. She continued, sensing her audience might help her persuade Luke: "I recently buried my mother, father, brother, and sister. Cholera. All their possessions—my memories of them—even our last family portrait—are in a trunk in my wagon. My clothes and every possession I have on earth, including my father's money, is in that wagon. Luke is heartless."

"Then," she continued, "my only living relative is waiting for me in San Francisco. Poor Aunt Hattie. She'll think I died, too!"

Quiet Aaron spoke first, "Luke is not heartless. Trust him; he doesn't make decisions on whims."

"Anyone can see," Jack put in, "that he cares about you."

Jared touched her arm. "Amanda, Luke thinks the world of you—perhaps if you spoke to him again. I know he'd never turn a deaf ear on someone in need."

Robert winked. "I'd have kidnapped you the first day I met you!"

Amanda sighed. No help here. They were certainly loyal to Luke.

"If you could have seen the girl you call Louise, you'd understand better, perhaps, what Luke saved you from. Took three days before that drug wore off enough for her to talk to us." Jared sighed. "Go talk to Luke. He has the world's biggest heart; I know he'll reconsider."

"If he doesn't," Robert said, "we'll help you."

"Agreed." They all chimed in.

Persuaded, Amanda sought Luke. She found him sitting by the creek, whittling a piece of wood with his knife.

They both spoke at once.

"Luke. . . ."

"Amanda. . . ."

They laughed, easing all tension between them.

"Sit down." Luke pointed to the log next to him. She sat beside him and watched him carve.

"Amanda," he began, "I'm sorry. At the time it was the only way out of a bad situation. I'm not sorry I got you away from there, but am sorry you were scared and sorry for the way I did it. Perhaps you were right; I should have confided in you. After all, you did prove to me you could be trusted. You didn't tell Charles or Ma about helping me that night with Louise."

"I forgive you," she whispered. "But you have to help me get back."

"No!"

"Luke," she pleaded. "Everything I own is on that train. All I have is this ragged nightdress. My family's possessions, the portrait, my money—"

"I've been thinking about that," Luke said. "If you go

back, they're going to want to know where you were. If your story doesn't hold, we lose our chance of finding Celia. Do you understand how important that is for us? We promised our parents we'd do everything we could to find her. She may not be alive, or she may be like Louise and need help right away."

"Luke, please . . ., you have brothers and other sisters. All I have of my family is in that trunk!"

"I know. . . ." He looked at her with sad eyes. "I want to help you. . . ." He sighed. "I've been trying to think of a way—"

"Jack and your brothers have agreed to help," she coaxed.

Luke touched her cheek and smiled. "Your begging wasn't necessary, you know. I'd made up my mind before you came down here that I'd get your things. I just have to figure out how." He scooped up his hair the way Phillip used to and smiled.

"But I can't rejoin the train?"

"I'm sorry. That's out of the question." Luke smacked his forehead with his hand. "Good gracious! Now I'm even sounding like a kidnapper!"

He turned, took Amanda's hands in his, and contemplated his words carefully before speaking: "Amanda, I kidnapped you. I did it to keep you from danger. I feared you wouldn't heed my warnings about Charles. However, now I feel like a criminal. . . . You need not ask permission for anything. I took you away from danger; I care what happens to you. I care very much. If you want to go back, I'll take you. I cannot hold you prisoner. But if you wish to stay with us, under our protection, I promise to bring back all your things—except the wagon."

Amanda studied him carefully. "Your brothers were right!"

He gave her a puzzled look.

She leaned over and kissed his cheek softly. "You *do* have the world's biggest heart! Thank you for saving me from Charles. Believe it or not, I had that very day changed my mind concerning him. I sensed his evilness."

"You weren't going to marry him?"

She shook her head. "I have to admit I was tempted by his charm and wealth. . . . Yet there was something I couldn't feel comfortable about with him."

Luke smiled boyishly at her words, and Amanda felt warmth surge through her chest.

"Then you won't go back?" Luke asked tensely.

She shook her head. "But couldn't I be of help there? I could spy on Charles and Ma for you."

"It's too dangerous for that now. I'd worry too much. I'd rather have you safely away from Charles. But I'm working on an idea—a way you can help us find Celia instead of going back to the ranch. Would you like that?"

"I'd gladly agree, if you could get my things."

He held out his hand. "A deal, let's shake on it!"

Amanda halted him. "One more thing. Is there any way you can give my wagon and supplies to Eliza and her family?"

"How can I? I'd have to admit I knew where you were to follow your instructions."

Amanda nodded, then wrinkled her brow as she began to think.

"Wait! What if I wrote a letter giving everything to Eliza? You could ride back with it and announce to the wagon train that I had been kidnapped by Indians, and you had rescued me, but I'd decided to go back to Ohio."

"Eliza?" he asked, puzzled.

"My friend. Remember, we often walked together?"

"The one with the baby?"

Amanda nodded.

"Hm-m, might work," he said. "It would also give me the opportunity to bring your personal possessions back to you. I'll quit my job with the train, too. My being away so much isn't fair to Larsen."

"What is your next plan for finding Celia?"

"I have an idea, but if I tell you, it will make you an accomplice. I want you out of this as much as possible."

"You remind me of Robin Hood."

Luke smiled. "I'll be gone for a day or two, and I'll probably take two of the men. Two will have to stay and protect my 'maid Marian.' Which two would you like?"

"I like them all."

Luke gave her a sheepish look. "Can I trust you with them?"

"Why, Luke, what do you mean? I won't hit them over their heads and steal their money."

Luke scooped his hair from his forehead and squinted. "You know what I mean."

"No, I don't. We're friends, and friends trust each other."

He squirmed uncomfortably. "Yes, but—"

"But, what?"

Luke held her face with both hands and looked into her eyes. "Amanda, you are so lovely—They—I—You just want to hear me say it, don't you?"

Puzzled, Amanda asked, "Say what?"

Luke stood suddenly and paced nervously before the log. Standing also, she followed his nervous steps, then darted directly in his path so he couldn't avoid her.

"What do you want to say?" she prompted.

He looked at her with such a forlorn expression that she took pity on him and put her arms around his neck and hugged him

Luke sighed and returned the hug with so much strength that Amanda broke the embrace with a laugh.

"You won't run off with Jared or Aaron if I leave them with you?"

"I assure you I will not. I sort of like *you*."

"You do?"

"I think," she whispered, "you are the very best friend I ever had."

"Best friend?"

"Yes. I appreciate the trouble you took to save me from Charles. I'm grateful, not angry at you for kidnapping me." She stood on tiptoes and kissed his lips. She'd only meant to peck his lips lightly, but they felt so warm and comfortable. When she did try to pull away, he put his arms around her and returned her kiss with a fervor that gave Amanda mixed feelings.

The next morning Luke set out for the wagon train. Amanda, Jared, and Aaron followed, staying about a mile south of its trail.

Amanda liked traveling with Luke's brothers. She rode one horse and led an unsaddled one behind her, as did the men. Jared had explained that they never traveled more than a hundred miles from their ranch without extra mounts.

One morning at breakfast Amanda asked Jared, "How many in your family?"

"Nine. Edward is our oldest brother. He's a preacher and is married to a saint named Caroline. He's the only one of us boys who's married, too. Two of the girls are, though. Edward and Caroline have no young uns yet.

"Emily is next; she's married and has three lively boys, John, Raymond, and Theo. By the time we get back, I may be an uncle again—not Emily though, but my next oldest sister, Sarah."

"Who's next?" Amanda asked, truly interested in Luke's family.

"Your favorite."

"Luke?" she asked.

"Yep. And he's single—at present that is. . . ."

"Oh? Is there someone back home who may change that?" Amanda asked quickly.

"Mercy, no. I was referring to your relationship. By the sudden whiteness of your face, I believe—"

"Come on, Jared, no fair. Who's next?"

"Yours truly is next. I'm single, but by Christmas I'll be tied tighter than a pickle barrel to Joanna." His look of tenderness told Amanda he missed her.

"Then," he continued, we have Elvira. She teaches school, is single, and will most likely remain that way if she doesn't stop being so fussy and stubborn. Every fella who courts, she finds fault with.

"Then there's Aaron and Robert—you've met them. They're both single. Lastly," Jared said sadly, "is our baby, Celia. Barely seventeen when she disappeared. I pray she's still alive."

"Sounds like a wonderful family," Amanda said. "I'd be proud, too."

Jared stood. "We have to hit the trail again, but at supper I want to hear about your family."

"Oh, you shall, for I'm proud, too!" replied Amanda.

On the second night Robert and Jack ran into camp just before Amanda bedded down in the tent. They were again dressed and painted like Indians and carried a rolled blanket.

"Sorry, Amanda," Robert announced, and he and Jack dropped the blanket inside her tent.

"Who is it?" Amanda asked, running to peek inside the bundle. "Ma!" she cried, untying her.

After a few oaths, Ma sat up and asked where she was and what was going on.

"It's a long story," Amanda stalled her.

"Where'd those Indians go? What are they planning to do with us? Have they hurt you, dear?" Ma asked, inserting oaths between her words.

Amanda flinched at each cuss word. How she wished Ma didn't swear so much.

"When the leader comes, he'll explain. In the meantime, let me assure you, your life is in no danger." Amanda wasn't sure how Luke wanted this handled.

At the sound of horses, Amanda peeked out of the tent. Luke rode into camp, pulling Robert and Jack's horses. He handed the reins to Aaron and headed for her tent.

"And how is our captive?" he greeted cheerfully.

Ma sat up and cussed Luke up and down, making Amanda and Luke both blush, then laugh, despite themselves.

"Ma, or whatever your name is, all I want is information. You cooperate, and I'll return you to Charles or wherever you want to go."

"I'm *Helen* to you," she snapped.

"Helen, then, have you ever seen this girl?" Luke held out a small oval painting inside a gold frame and covered in glass.

Amanda could hardly wait for Helen to finish looking at the painting so she could see it.

Helen's face turned white. "Might have. Who is she?"

"My sister, Celia. I must find her. Can you help me?"

Helen continued to stare at the picture.

"Well, have you ever seen her?" Luke asked impatiently.

"I'm thinkin'," Ma snapped. "I mighta. People change," she added in a small, faint voice.

"What's wrong?" Amanda asked, noticing Helen's pal ing face. Ma began cursing again, mostly about the rotten business and what people have to do to make money

"Ma," pleaded Amanda, "if you know anything that will help Luke, please tell him. He'll let you go. I promise."

"Otherwise?" she asked, squinting at Luke with distrust.

"Otherwise," Luke replied, "you travel to Texas, where my mother will make a real lady, a Christian lady, out of you."

After another string of curses, mainly concerning getting to Frisco and her business, she asked, "If I tell you what I know, it may damage my business partner. What will happen to him? No sense going to Frisco if I don't have half a business or a partner."

"You'll have it all," Luke said simply.

"I will?"

"If your partner is arrested, then you'll own it all, unless he has made other stipulations."

"I'll own the whole thing?"

"If you run it legally. Otherwise you could end up with Charles, behind bars or hanged."

Helen shivered "All right, I'll tell you what I know "

8

*L*uke called Aaron, Jared, Robert, and Jack into the small tent. Everyone was silent. All eyes rested on Helen. She sat Indian style, her long brown taffeta pulled tightly over her knees. She smoothed the stray hairs from her swept-up hairdo and adjusted her bracelets, seemingly enjoying the attention, or else stalling for time. Amanda noticed that this was the first time she'd seen Helen without her makeup; she looked much better without it, almost motherly

"We want to know where our sister is, said Luke

"She's on one of the wagons ahead of ours," Helen stated matter-of-factly

"Is she all right?" Robert and Luke both asked at once

Helen squirmed a bit. "I guess she is. I haven't seen her but once or twice, when she first came to us.'

Relief that Celia was alive spread over the faces of the men. Suddenly Luke's face turned bitter as he asked gruffly, "Is she drugged?'

After muttering curses beneath her breath, Helen finally admitted, "Yes, since the first night. Bella said she was in poor shape." She glanced at the worried looks and added, "But alive!"

Luke stood and paced, "How many guarding her?"

"Far as I know, just two women, Luella and Tina," Helen said.

"Think some Indians might attack tonight, Luke?" asked Robert with a grin.

"Doesn't sound like we have too much time to waste. Let's go!" Luke opened the tent flap to let the men out. He turned back and faced Amanda. "I'll leave Aaron with you. Try to get some sleep. We may need help with Celia if we find her."

Amanda nodded.

"We'll be praying the whole time we're riding." He looked at her sadly. "I'd ask you to pray, too, but you still aren't talking to God, are you?"

"He didn't listen when I prayed for Mama or Pa. Why should He listen if I pray for Celia?"

"He'll listen, but we can't demand He do what *we* want Him to. We have to merely ask—beg sometimes. Yet we have to leave the final decision to Him, and the hardest part is accepting that decision, even if it isn't the one we wanted."

"I'll try," Amanda said in a small, unsure voice.

"Promise?" Luke whispered.

"Promise."

He smiled and was gone. Moments later she heard them ride away. Helen had already fallen asleep. Amanda drew up her knees, hugged them, and prayed for the first time since her family died. She felt awkward after such a long time, but in several moments, the words flowed almost like old times. She prayed in earnest that the kind brothers would find their beloved sister, and if it be His will, she be alive. Her prayer may have been slightly awkward and short, but it was sincere, and Amanda felt peaceful afterwards. Rolled in her blanket, feeling closer to her Maker than she had in many weeks, she fell asleep.

The smell of coffee aroused Amanda. Her stomach churned, reminding her she hadn't eaten much the day before, and now she was extremely hungry. Crawling over Helen's sleeping form, she followed the smells outside to where Aaron had a fire and a pot of coffee brewing.

"What's that?" she asked pointing to a slab of freshly cleaned game.

"Rabbit."

"Breakfast?"

He nodded and smiled. "Sorry, no eggs and bacon."

"I love rabbit."

"You do?"

"Never had it for breakfast before, but Pa used to hunt, and we ate wild game all the time. My favorite is venison."

He handed her a cup of hot coffee. "It will be a while before our rabbit is ready."

She sipped the coffee gingerly. It was hot but delicious. "How long do you think it will take Luke and the men to find Celia?"

"Depends on how far they have to ride to find the right train."

"Will we wait here or move with them?"

"Luke said to wait this time."

Amanda liked Aaron but found conversation with him difficult, as he was so quiet and wasted no words. He wasn't rude, for what he did say was softly spoken and kind. Yet she wasn't sure if she should try to draw him into further conversation or leave him alone. So she sat quietly with her coffee and decided to follow his lead.

After several moments he surprised her by asking frankly, "Do you know God?"

"Sort of," she answered.

"No such thing. You either know Him or you don't."

"It's a long story. I come from a Bible-reading family, a praying family. When I lost them, I gave up on God and prayer. I know what you're going to say—Luke said it all. It's just that my wounds are still unhealed. It will take time, I guess. I prayed for Celia last night. I promised Luke I would."

He studied her carefully. He didn't lecture her as she had expected. "Ah-h, you promised Luke." He chuckled. It was the first time he'd done more than smile since she'd met him.

"Why do you care?"

"Because I love Luke."

"And . . . ," she prompted.

"In case . . . , if you and he . . . ," he fumbled for words.

"We're close friends, that's all."

"You sure?"

"I'm not ready for a commitment in my life. I need to get my belongings and find a way to San Francisco and Aunt Hattie."

"Luke brought back your things. They were strapped to the two extra horses. I put them behind your tent."

Amanda breathed a sigh of relief. "Thank goodness. Now, I just have to figure out a way to San Francisco."

Aaron shook his head. "I guess if you want to go that badly, Helen will take you. But I warn you, she's not the type a girl like you should associate with. So I guess it depends on how badly you want to go. I'd hate to think of what you may become or appear to become in her company."

*   *   *

Amanda sorted through her belongings. All her possessions and those of her family were intact. She washed in the small creek and put on a clean blue cotton dress with a white apron. By the time she returned, Helen was awake and drinking coffee with Aaron. Amanda noticed they talked intently, so she bypassed them and went to her tent. She folded bedding and straightened up, all the while thinking of how she'd get to San Francisco and Aunt Hattie.

Helen entered the tent, holding out a cup of coffee.

"Here, honey, Aaron said to finish off the coffee so he can clean the pot." She held a cup for herself in her other hand. Helen plopped down upon the folded blankets. "So you're in with these men, are you?"

"I was kidnapped, like you," Amanda replied carefully, sitting down beside her.

"But now you're in with them?" she asked, raising her eyebrows suspiciously

"I suppose I am, now that I know the truth about you and Charles and what you had planned for me and the other girls. Especially after what you did to Louise and Celia."

Helen cursed before admitting, "I never felt good about that part. I preferred to use willing girls. That was all Charles's doing. I tried to talk him out of that business, but. . . ." She took a long sip from her cup. "Anyway, I always treated my girls good."

Amanda smiled. Despite her faults, Helen was a likable lady. "You treated me well. I liked you. We would have gotten along, if—"

"We still could!" Helen exclaimed excitedly. She reached over and squeezed Amanda's arm. "The business will be all mine. I can run it the way I want. I promise not to use any tricks. I'll use only willing girls, like Bella. I can make you rich, honey."

"You're still going to San Francisco then?"

"Of course. Didn't that Luke fella say I could rejoin the train, if I talked?"

"Yes. If your information was true."

"It was. Come with me, Amanda, you'll be my number-one girl."

Amanda jerked away from Helen. "In a brothel!"

Helen looked down at her hands. "You wouldn't have to be a part of that. You could just be a hostess or even my guest."

Amanda gazed at Helen with sympathy. Their lives were so different, yet Helen was a person with feelings, too. Helen's life had probably been a sad one. Amanda tried to be gentle. "I want to go to San Francisco, but not in the company of . . . of . . . ," Amanda fumbled for the word.

"Saloon women?" Helen offered.

"Yes," she answered. "I don't approve of brothels or your hotel."

"If you change your mind—"

"I won't," Amanda stated positively.

Helen stood. "That Aaron said he'd ride me back to the train. Won't you at least come back to your wagon and continue to California?"

"You remember my friend Eliza from the train? The one with the baby? I gave everything to her and her husband in a letter that Luke delivered before they kidnapped you. In that letter I stated my intentions to return to Ohio and not continue to California. I've since decided I will continue to California, but not with the train."

"How then?"

"I don't know. But I'll get there."

Helen looked at her apologetically. "Will you look me up?"

Amanda looked down at her lap. "I'm sorry, Helen. As long as you're in that type of business, I cannot."

"What's wrong with a little drinking, gambling, and dancing? Those fellas need a little fun. It's harmless."

"Is it? What about Louise? And Celia? And how many others like them? What about the men who drink too much or gamble away all their earnings? What about morals and being God fearing?" Amanda stopped to take a breath. She had more to say, but Helen interrupted.

"Oh, no, not another sermon! Aaron already preached to me. I couldn't take another Bible lesson." She shook her head sadly. "But you know, he almost had me when he told me Jesus loved me. Nobody ever loved me. He had tears in his eyes. Real tears, when he told me." Her voice softened so that Amanda could barely recognize it. "I almost believed him. Somebody loving me! That's a laugh."

Amanda's heart went out to Helen. She'd never seen her so soft or vulnerable.

"Why do you think no one could love you?" Amanda asked. "I did until—"

"Until you discovered how wicked I am; that's the story of my life. No one ever cared what I did or how I behaved. Whenever someone came close to loving me, there was always some little thing about me that stopped them.

"When I was sixteen, I fell in love. I thought he loved me, too. I was so sure. Then when I suggested marriage, he laughed. I wasn't good enough. I was from the wrong side of the hill. He kept saying, 'If only, if only you weren't from under the hill.' " Helen explained, "That's what they called the district of Savannah where I lived—the wharf area. My mother was a 'window waver'—a prostitute who waved sailors up to her room from her window facing the docks. My father was one of the many who answered her wave."

It had never dawned on Amanda that women like Helen had pasts and unhappy childhoods. How ignorant of her. Of course they didn't have loving families as she and Luke did. How could she be so quick to judge? She touched Helen's hand. "I'm sorry. . . ."

Helen shook off her melancholy mood. "Don't be, honey, it made me tough. I survived. I don't need anyone; I can make it alone. I have a nice place in Frisco—and money, too!"

Amanda thought about how close she had come to giving up her ideals for Charles and his money. What good was money without love? Everyone needs to be loved by someone.

"*I* love you, Helen," Amanda squeezed out in a squeaky voice filled with emotion.

Helen hugged Amanda. "You came close, honey. You were special to me, too."

"Don't go back to the train and Frisco," Amanda pleaded "I have to, honey, it's the only life I know."

Amanda excused herself from the tent and searched for Aaron. She found him washing dishes in the creek.

"I would have helped you, had you asked," she offered.

"I don't mind," he replied as he shined the old coffeepot with a rag.

"Did you tell Helen you'd ride her back to the train?"

"Yes, but it never dawned on me that I can't."

"Why?"

"I can't leave you alone, and Luke would kill me if I took you anywhere near that train "

"Good."

"Good? Why?" He asked with curious eyes.

"Helen told me about the talk you and she had. She said you almost had her when you told her Jesus loved her. Aaron, that's her weak point. This will give you more time to convince her that God does care about her. She claims no one has ever loved her "

"Why don't you convince her?" he asked.

"Me? I-I can't!"

"Why? You believe it, don't you?" His eyes pierced hers until she was forced to look away.

"I'm still faltering myself. How can I convince someone else?"

"Why would you want me to convince Helen of something you weren't sure of yourself?"

Confused and uncomfortable with being questioned on such a sore subject, Amanda turned her tearing face from Aaron and fled back to the tent.

9

*T*he fire had Amanda momentarily mesmerized. A log suddenly shifted, and the fire crackled. Her body jumped slightly as she was rudely pulled from her daze. She looked across the fire at Aaron and Helen. All she could see of them was their faces; everything else blended into the darkness of the night. They usually listened to Aaron tell stories of the ranch and family, but lately their evenings by the fire had become quiet. Luke and the men had been gone for over a week. Had something happened to them? To Celia?

Aaron had spent much time with Helen during the week, but neither discussed their conversations with Amanda, so she didn't know what they had talked about. Helen had been helpful and cheerful and hadn't mentioned San Francisco or the hotel again. She also seemed as concerned for Luke, the men, and Celia as she and Aaron were.

"Tired, Amanda?" Helen yawned.

She nodded. "Must have been all the laundry we washed."

Helen stood. "Come, let's turn in then. Maybe tomorrow we'll—"

"Sh-h-h!" Aaron hissed, standing with his head cocked

Both women froze

Somewhere a coyote howled and an owl hooted. Amanda shivered despite the fire. What did Aaron hear? Something dangerous?

"Get ready to douse the fire," he ordered, running toward the nearby brush. "I'll whistle three times like this," he demonstrated his call, "then douse it and run to where the horses are hidden and wait for me " He turned and disappeared into the bushes

"I-I'm scared, Helen," Amanda shivered again

"Me, too, and I don't scare easily," Helen whispered

"What do you think Aaron heard?"

Helen shrugged. "I didn't hear anything unusual."

They stood with arms wrapped around each other for several moments before Helen surprised Amanda.

"Wanna say a prayer?" she asked timidly.

"Together? I'm not sure I can, I'm too frightened," Amanda said.

"But you've probably done it before. I never have." She hesitated. "Never would have thought of it, except Aaron's been putting notions in my head."

"Aaron's extremely smart," Amanda said, taking Helen's hand. "All right, here goes," she whispered. Amanda asked God for protection in simple words, and both said, "Amen," moments before riders on horses burst through the brush toward their fire.

It was moments before Amanda recognized Luke, Robert, Jared, and Jack. Aaron carried a blanket close to the fire and everyone closed in around them. It was Celia.

The figure in the blanket looked like a mere child, the bundle was so slight. As Amanda moved closer she could see the girl was extremely thin and white. Luke motioned her even closer, whispering softly, "Can you help her, Amanda?"

Basic instinct made Amanda rush to the girl's side and feel her forehead and loosen her clothing to make her comfortable.

Celia was barely conscious and weak. Once Amanda had examined her and made her comfortable, she was at a loss as to how to help the girl. Surprisingly, that's when Helen took over.

"Aaron, get her into our tent," she ordered. "You, Helen pointed at Robert, "bring some drinking water." To Luke she said, "Get her something soft to eat—berries, something. . . . Helen rushed into the tent behind Aaron, who carried Celia. "I'll need your help, too, Amanda," she called over her shoulder.

Amanda helped Helen feed Luke's sister. Celia fought but was too weak to cause a threat to Helen and Amanda's determination that she eat. Afterwards, Celia fell into an exhausted sleep.

"She's so beautiful," exclaimed Amanda as she smoothed Celia's tangled and matted blond hair "She looks like a china doll."

"And just as fragile," Helen muttered. "I knew this one wouldn't make it. I tried to warn Charles .   " She swore mildly beneath her breath.

"You think she won't make it?" Amanda gasped in horror

"I meant make it to San Francisco. She's weak and is probably suffering from malnutrition—but she might pull through. I wish we had some oranges or orange juice. She needs fruit. These berries Luke found might do the trick Look like raspberries, and it's about their season."

"Amanda?" A male voice called her softly from outside the tent

She peeked out

"How is she?" Luke whispered.

"Weak."

"The boys and I are praying. .

Amanda, recalling her prayers when her family ailed, changed the subject. "Listen, you and the men have ridden for days. Why don't you get some rest? Helen and I will take turns watching Celia."

"Thank you," he whispered and was gone

Amanda took the first shift with Celia while Helen slept on a blanket nearby. The girl slept fitfully, sometimes grabbing Amanda's hand fiercely as if in fright. Each time Amanda soothed her back into a peaceful slumber.

After a few hours, Helen woke, and they fed Celia again Once Celia fell asleep, Amanda curled up in the blanket and took her turn at slumber

Amanda still could not understand how she slept through all the commotion that must have ensued that next morning shortly before dawn.

She awoke mid-morning, and it took her several seconds to recall where she was and what had transpired the previous evening. She immediately focused her eyes to Celia's mat, but the girl was not there, and neither was Helen

Still dressed in her blue-and-white gingham of the day before, Amanda rushed out of the tent. She stood frozen by the sight that met her. The bundle lay once more by the fire, but this time the blanket completely covered the figure inside. Everyone stood with heads bowed and grief-stricken faces. Amanda knew Celia was dead.

Amanda walked toward the woods, found a seat upon a dead log, and cried. Poor Celia. So young and beautiful. She could have known such happiness. Amanda looked upward. *Why?*

Sitting upon her log for most of the afternoon, Amanda watched the brothers grieve for their baby sister, mixing their crying with prayers. *What did I do when my family died?* Amanda puzzled. *I prayed, then mourned, then refused to pray ever again.* The memory of her own recent grief brought on a while new flood of tears.

Amanda also worried about Helen. What would happen to her now? Because of her involvement with the man responsible for the death of their sister, surely they would not accept her. Helen had just begun to confide in God. What would this do to her newfound faith? Where would Helen go?

The men held a service for Celia and buried her beneath a large cottonwood tree. Jared carved a cross for the grave, and they placed large rocks to cover over the mound to keep the wolves away.

Everyone was quiet that day, including Helen and Amanda. Sitting sedately in their tent that evening, Helen asked, "What happens now?"

"I don't know," Amanda said carefully, fearing what might be next.

"I did the best I could to save her . . . ," Helen cried softly.

"Of course you did! It wasn't your fault," soothed Amanda.

"Oh, how wrong you are, Amanda," sighed Helen tearfully. "I'm as guilty as Charles. If I couldn't stop him, I should have quit. I never realized—*their sister is dead!*"

Amanda watched strong, tough Helen bury her face in her hands and weep. Amanda embraced the sobbing older woman's shoulders and squeezed her gently. It was the only comfort she could offer. She was speechless.

Between sobs, Helen managed to ask, "What will the men do to me now? Will they kill me, as Charles's accomplice? Will they leave me here to die? Will they hate me? Oh, Amanda I'm truly sorry—will they believe me? Will they forgive me?"

"I don't know," Amanda said truthfully. "I just don't know." She had no idea how the brothers would react to the death of their sister. Recalling the loss she'd felt when her loved ones died, she shivered and dreaded the thought of their reaction.

In the morning, both women remained in their tent after bathing and dressing. Unsure of the reaction to Celia's death, they thought it best to stay out of the men's sight. They were stunned when Aaron called outside their tent, "Aren't you gals going to eat breakfast? It'll be a long time until lunch—better get out here fast!"

Helen and Amanda exchanged surprised glances.

"We'll be right out!" Amanda called.

Helen smoothed the collar of Amanda's pink cotton dress. "Well, here goes."

"It'll be all right," Amanda comforted with more confidence than she felt.

Amanda hoped it would be like old times, and just Aaron would be eating with them, but all greeted them at the fire. The women sat and accepted the fresh fish and coffee offered them.

"Are you ladies ready to travel?" Luke asked, trying to sound casual.

Amanda noticed his red eyes and tired face. He grieved yet seemed ready to carry on as usual.

"Travel?" they both chimed.

"Helen," Luke turned to address her singly. Amanda saw Helen cringe and look up, as if dreading his next words. "I will escort you to the wagon train, though it may take a few days to catch up. We'll leave as soon as you've finished," he said kindly.

Helen merely stared at him.

He turned to Amanda, and his eyes softened noticeably. "We'll escort you back to our ranch. From there you may choose where you'd like to go. We'll help you get there. I'll catch up as soon as I take Helen back to the train."

"Listen here," Helen countered. "Will you force me to go where I don't choose to go?"

Luke spun around, "I beg your pardon?"

"I've changed my mind. I don't want to go back to the train. I prefer to stay with Amanda. May I?" she added meekly.

Luke glanced back and forth from Amanda to Helen for several seconds before smiling. "You may, and I'm happy with your decision. However, this will cause a change in our plans and a slight delay to our start. I'll converse with the men and decide our plans. Excuse me, ladies." He turned to his brothers and Jack. "A short meeting. Be at the creek in five minutes."

They all nodded.

When the men were gone, Amanda shook her head in disbelief. "I can't believe how they are handling this whole situation. They are grieving, but still functioning normally. The most surprising thing of all is they have no hard feelings toward you at all! I can't understand how they can react this way!"

"You could have knocked me over . . . , I'll tell you! I thought for sure Luke was gonna ride me out on a pole, with tar and feathers!" exclaimed Helen.

"And," Amanda continued, "*your* decision jolted me! I'm thrilled but never expected so many surprises in one morning!"

Helen sobered. "I couldn't go back to that life after what I've heard and seen this past week. Not just Celia, but Aaron's sermons have really made me think."

"Everything," Amanda sighed, "this morning has made me think."

The men returned, and Luke announced their plans. "There is something I need to do. I'll be riding in a different direction for a week or two, but I'll catch up long before you reach the ranch. I don't dare take away any more men, so I'll travel alone." Luke looked at Amanda and Helen. "One thing I must ask. Please cooperate fully with my brothers and Jack. The trip should be safe. They know the land well, but obey them at all times, because there are dangers."

"Indians?" Helen asked calmly.

"Yes, as well as snakes, wild animals, and desperadoes—" Seeing Amanda's face pale, he added, "Just trust the men and obey them at all times, and you have nothing to fear. They've traveled this area numerous times and know every inch by heart. Just do as they say, and none of us will have to worry." He smiled and winked. "Amanda, may I see you down by the creek before I leave?"

Luke held out his hands for hers as she approached, but somehow their hands became forgotten, and they embraced each other tightly.

"I missed you," he whispered.

She drew away from him slightly. "I'm sorry about Celia—I did pray, as I promised. It didn't do any good this time either."

Luke frowned and drew her down beside him on the creek bank.

"That isn't so. We prayed that God's will be done. He wanted Celia. We accept that and even thank Him."

"Thank Him!" Amanda gasped in confusion.

"Yes. He could have taken her before we had a chance to rescue her. She might have died alone on that train, among strangers. Helen called us all in when she realized . . . , and Celia left earth embraced by her brothers. Things could have been so different. She even smiled. . . ." He turned his head quickly. "We loved her, and we'll miss her, but we know exactly where she is—in the best of hands."

"Luke, that's so beautiful . . . , and you hold no resentment toward Helen?"

"No, we have to forgive as God forgives us."

"What about Charles?" she asked.

"Now that's another matter. While we have forgiven him, we believe justice must be done. He cannot be free to harm others. That's the business I must settle. I need to find a lawman who'll help me see justice done. That train is pretty far by now, so that won't be easy. First I'll find the train, then head for the nearest town that has a lawman." He hesitated, taking her hand, "If that isn't possible, I'll have to get Larsen and some of the other men to help me tie him to a horse so I can ride him to the law."

She touched his hand. "Be careful, Luke."

He gazed at her seriously. "You still planning to go to San Francisco and Aunt Hattie?"

Amanda's heart pounded. *Why did he ask that in such a way that I know he wants a negative answer?* Even the pleading look in his eyes told her he wanted her to say no. Amanda cringed. His eyes, still red in grief for his sister, pleaded for something she was unable to give him. Despite her growing fondness for him, she must fulfill her family's dream.

"Yes."

"Can I give you an alternative to consider?"

"No, please don't!" She stood. He rose also and started to speak, but she put her finger to his lips. "Just make sure you meet us safely, long before we reach the ranch. Just because I still want to go to San Francisco doesn't mean I don't care what happens to you."

He touched her cheek. "I will. And you be careful, too."

"Friends can hug, can't they? Especially when they're about to be separated?" she asked, her eyes anxious.

"You bet," he laughed, taking her into his arms and embracing her tightly. "But can they kiss, too?"

She answered by giving him her lips.

10

*T*raveling on horseback, while faster, had its draw-
backs, as Amanda discovered early on their trip to the
Sterling ranch. Summer had faded into early fall, and the
mornings and nights turned cold. When it rained, the riders
became extremely wet. The brush at times was thick and
scratched limbs and sometimes faces if the riders weren't
careful enough to duck quickly. The men faired better, in
their ranch clothing of sturdy pants, flannel shirts, high
boots, and wide-brimmed flannel hats. The women were
encumbered with long dresses, petticoats, and flimsy cotton bonnets. They had to ride astride, as there were no
sidesaddles.

The men teased them sometimes, but also complimented
their persistence and endurance under such adverse conditions and admired their stamina.

The women admired the men also. They knew exactly
where they were going, though neither woman could figure out how they could possibly know where they were

The scenery looked the same, and often they traveled without even following a path. They listened to every sound cautiously and knew where every possible danger hid.

The men wore holsters at their waists, with six-shooters ready at all times to be swung into service, as on the day when a rattlesnake entered their camp area. Jared fired and killed it before the ladies knew it was there.

One night the men heard a noise and ordered them to douse the fire. They then silently watched three men ride within several hundred feet of their camp. Aaron explained that they might have been harmless, but it was always best to be careful. The West was full of what they called desperadoes, especially since the beginning of the Gold Rush.

The women felt safe with the Sterling brothers and Jack. Heeding Luke's warning, they obeyed them without question.

Every evening after supper, by the light of the campfire, the men held devotions and read from a Bible. During the closing prayer one night a noise brought an abrupt "amen" from the men, and they hushed everyone to listen to the sound.

Amanda tried to concentrate on which noise they were listening to. The coyote? The howling of a wolf? The owl's hoot? These had all become commonplace and sounded no different from usual. Yet the men listened carefully for several minutes before exchanging looks of glee. They slapped each other on their backs and cheered.

"What is it?" Amanda asked.

"One of us," Jared replied. "It's either Luke or Edward."

"But I don't hear anything," Amanda said with frustration.

Jared came to stand beside her. "Hear the owl?" he asked.

She nodded

"Listen carefully to its hoots. A three, a two, and a three, then five seconds of silence, and another set of three, two and three, five seconds of silence—and he'll keep it up until one of us answers with sets of two, three, and two hoots." He turned to Robert, "Give the signal. You do it best."

Robert gave the owl hoots for a good fifteen minutes at the timed intervals.

"How long does he have to keep hooting?" Amanda asked.

"Until Luke or Edward can follow the call, catch sight of our fire, and locate us," Jared explained. "We've been doing this for years. Our father taught us at a young age, in case we ever got lost while hunting."

"Do you think it's Luke?" she asked.

"Luke or Edward."

"Edward?"

"Our oldest brother, the minister who escorted 'Louise' back to the ranch. He may have decided to come back and help us. Or it could be Luke. . . ." Jared looked closely at Amanda. "Why are you smiling with shiny, bright eyes? Are you excited by the thought of Luke returning?"

Amanda wondered how Jared always managed to see her true feelings. She'd have to hide them better. "You sound like Robert with your teasing. Yes, I can't wait to see my friend again. Friends can miss each other, can't they?" she asked.

"There are plenty of girls in Texas who will be glad you and he are just friends," he teased.

"I'm glad I can make half the state happy," she replied.

Amanda wondered why Luke's brothers seemed to doubt that she and Luke were only friends, yet when Luke rode into camp, moments later, she questioned it herself.

Perched behind him on the saddle sat a young woman with her arms around Luke's waist. As they rode closer to the fire and the brothers greeted him warmly, all Amanda could do was stare at the shapely, beautiful woman

Her long red hair bounced with the gait of the horse, and her large eyes scanned the gathering quickly. When they came to rest on Amanda, sparks filled the night air

Luke dismounted and helped the woman from the horse and brought her to where Amanda and Helen sat

"Amanda, Helen, I want you to meet—," Luke began

"Ruby Ziegler!" exclaimed Helen

"You two have met then?" Luke asked

"A few times. She was traveling with us in one of the trains ahead," Helen said in a manner that left Amanda to believe she was leaving out something important.

Luke continued, "And this, Ruby, is my good friend Amanda Barker "

Amanda flashed Luke a fiery look Had he emphasized the word *friend,* or had Amanda merely imagined it?

The women nodded cautiously at one another.

As Luke introduced her to his brothers and Jack, Amanda noticed her petite form and Luke's hand resting on her tiny waist as he led her around the campfire.

To Amanda's chagrin, Ruby was to sleep in the already crowded small tent with Helen and herself. This gave Amanda no chance to question Helen about Ruby. What troubled Amanda was she knew why Ruby's arrival upset her. What troubled her more was why was the feeling apparently mutual? Had Ruby already fallen victim to Luke's irresistible charm? *But why should I care?* she asked herself. *My friendship with Luke is secondary to fulfilling my family's dream of reaching San Francisco and Aunt Hattie.* She vowed to guard her feelings.

It wasn't until late morning of the next day that Luke approached Amanda. Her horse had fallen a bit behind the others, and Luke rode back and joined her.

"Miss me?" he grinned, scooping his hair from his eyes.
"You were away?" she teased.

He laughed heartily and purposely loud, Amanda thought, for Ruby riding ahead several yards turned their way and frowned.

Luke sobered and gazed at Amanda for several moments. "I missed you." When she didn't answer, he continued, "I have important news. Let's ride ahead so we can stop and talk."

He galloped ahead, and she followed. She felt Ruby's eyes scorching her as she passed out of view. They rode several miles ahead of the others and stopped beside a huge rock, dismounted, and perched upon it.

Luke's eyes searched hers tenderly. "My news may come as a great shock to you. Are you prepared?"

She looked at him, her fear apparent. She closed her eyes. *Prepared?* Her skin tingled.

"Oh, Luke, what now?"

"I found Charles. He's dead."

Her eyes popped open. "Dead? How?"

He took a deep breath. "I found Larsen's wagon train just west of Fort Bridger. They were all killed by Indians. Charles, Larsen, Griff, Bella, the Elliotts, the Simpsons—"

"My friend Eliza and her family?" Amanda asked with a shudder.

"No. I was told the train split at Fort Bridger. Those going to Oregon went north, those going to California, west. Because they had your wagon and extra supplies they decided to go all the way to Oregon instead. You saved their lives!"

"Thank God!" she breathed.

"When I got there, another wagon train had just arrived, and the men were burying the dead. It was an awful sight. I saw Charles dead with my own eyes, so I'm sure he won't bother any more innocent girls. As it happened, the train that was behind them and was now burying the dead had originally been several trains ahead. The train's captain had been ill, and they lost a few days, so that probably saved them. That's how I found Ruby. She was another of Charles's innocent victims. She was with two other girls who decided to continue to San Francisco; Ruby preferred to go back home. So I brought her with me."

"She's very beautiful," Amanda said, watching Luke carefully.

"One thing I'll say for Charles: He had good taste. He knew exactly the type of girl that would make him rich in Frisco." Luke saddened. "Celia was beautiful, too."

"She reminded me of a fragile china doll," Amanda said.

Luke jumped down and held out his hand. "You'll give Helen the news?"

Amanda nodded, taking his hand absently.

As he pulled her gently to the ground he asked, "Is something wrong, Amanda?"

"I was just thinking about our wagon train," she said, eyes tearing. "God *did* hear and answer my prayers!"

"Of course He did! What made you realize it?"

She sniffed and wiped her eyes. "My family could have died violent, terrifying deaths at the hands of the Indians, but He spared them that. He let them die peacefully and naturally. Then he allowed me to get mixed up with Charles, so you would kidnap me, and my life was spared. He didn't ignore my prayers! He does love me!"

"I won't say it, you know," Luke brushed her tears away with his finger.

"Won't say what?" She sniffled.

"*I told you so!*"

Amanda buried her head in the breast of his shirt and cried, "I need a hug!"

He squeezed her to him. "You got it!" He then held her at arm's length and smiled. "After all, what are friends for?"

That night after supper, while Ruby sat by the fire, listening to Robert and Jared's stories, and Luke, Jack, and Aaron were caring for the horses, Amanda signaled Helen into their tent.

Sitting on her blanket and patting the space beside her, "Sit down, Helen," Amanda invited. "I have some shocking news."

"What is it?" Helen wondered aloud, eyes wide.

Amanda retold the tale of the wagon train as Luke had earlier that day.

"Charles dead? I can't believe it!" she kept repeating. "Good gracious! If I hadn't decided to stay with you and clean up my life. . . . If it hadn't been for Celia. . . . I'd have been on that train, too!"

"Really makes you think, doesn't it? We have a lot to be thankful for."

Helen shook her curly red head. "I never put much thought to God and such, and now already miracles are happening to me. I feel loved for the first time in my life. He saved a wicked gal like me in more ways than one!" She cast her eyes upward, "Thank You, Lord. I'll try, from now on, to be worthy of Your love."

"Amen," whispered Amanda. After several seconds of silence, Amanda said, "Helen, may I ask you about Ruby?"

Helen smiled and winked knowingly. "I wondered how long it would take. I'd have been disappointed if you hadn't asked."

"Why?" Amanda tipped her head curiously.

"I could see that her presence bothered you, and I've been dying to give you advice about it."

"You noticed? I don't understand why I feel animosity toward her, I really don't."

"Could it be because of Luke?" When Amanda didn't answer, but merely shrugged, Helen patted her hand. "You needn't answer, but let me assure you, Ruby is not Luke's type. She has him completely fooled. She came with us of her own free will; she wasn't coerced. She was a saloon girl in Saint Louis, and she's aware that I know it. She continually gives me warning looks and tries to butter me up to keep me silent. She offered to do my laundry this morning! Of course I refused."

"But she's so pretty and vivacious." Amanda sighed. 'All the men dote on her, including Luke. He's my friend. I'd not want to see him hurt is all."

"Luke isn't stupid. He isn't even attracted to her. It's just flattery for him. And she isn't half as lovely as you are! Her beauty isn't natural like yours. Look at all the makeup she spreads on every morning." Helen shook her head, "I tell you you're worried for no reason. Luke is kind to Ruby, but has eyes only for you. Even an old maid like me can see that!"

Helen eyed Amanda suspiciously. "I also think your interest in Luke is beyond friendship. You can't fool me."

"I'm not trying to fool you. I'm just confused about my feelings. My only concern is to find a way to California. I don't have room in my plans for anything more than friendship."

Helen pinched Amanda's cheeks gently. "I think you should examine your priorities. You'll be mighty lonely in Frisco if your feelings for Luke are as I suspect they are."

Helen's words reflected exactly what Amanda's recent thoughts had been. "Is it possible to have both? Luke and San Francisco?" Amanda wrung her hands nervously. "Oh, Helen, what should I do?"

"Let Luke know you think of him as more than just a friend. He needs encouragement."

"I don't know how to do that." Amanda looked up at Helen quickly and exclaimed in a panicky voice, "You won't say anything to him, will you?"

Helen took Amanda's hands in hers. "You can always trust me. Not only is your secret safe, I'll do anything I can to help. I'm proud that you confided in me."

Amanda threw her arms around Helen. "I'm so glad things worked out as they did. I'm happy you changed and came with me."

"Me, too!" Helen laughed. "Especially since I heard what happened to our wagon train!"

At first Helen had balked at wearing the two dresses belonging to Amanda's mother that Amanda had dug from the clothing Luke rescued from her wagon. "They aren't my style," Helen objected as she examined them. However, after a week in the same dress, she had begun wearing them just while her dress was being laundered. Now of course, with the rips and tears the rugged terrain had made in her clothes she wore the practical dresses and was thankful for them. More and more Amanda noticed the dresses no longer looked foreign on her, for every day Helen became increasingly like those dresses.

Since hearing about Larsen's wagon train, Amanda had changed, too. Her prayers were no longer strained. Her relationship with God had returned to a sure footing.

Amanda's only battle now was her feelings for Luke. What she wished was only friendship began to feel much stronger, especially when Ruby was around. *What is love?* she wondered. *That thrill and goose bumpy feeling I got whenever Charles touched me? Or the warm glow I feel whenever I'm*

*around Luke? That can't be—I always thought it was mere broth-
erly love or friendship.*

There was little time for socializing as they traveled, for
the Sterlings were all business. Their objective was to get to
the ranch safely, and they concentrated fully on that. The
after-supper fireside was the only opportunity to get to
know one another. The men seemed to enjoy telling Ruby
stories and joking with her. Amanda knew Ruby's beauty
attracted them, but she also had an ability to make them feel
masculine. Ruby had the art of flirting down pat. Though
Amanda vowed to like Ruby, it became harder as she mo-
nopolized not only all the other men's attention, but Luke's,
too.

11

Amanda bit her upper lip and tried to smile as she rode past Ruby and Luke to reach Helen's side. She always rode beside Helen. Ruby began the day riding with the women but always managed to lag behind so she could be near Luke or Robert, who took turns riding at the rear of the traveling party

Helen took in Amanda's forced smile and motioned with her facial expression for Amanda to follow her. Helen turned her horse to the right, and Amanda followed. She led her to the side a few hundred yards so they could talk without being overheard by Luke and Ruby behind or the other men ahead.

"Ruby getting on your nerves again?" Helen asked.

"It's my fault. It shouldn't bother me. But doesn't Luke realize how she irks me?" Amanda asked. "He could put a stop to her flirting if he wanted to. He must be enjoying it!"

Helen hesitated before saying, "It's none of my business,

but isn't it possible that he's allowing it on purpose, just to see if you care?"

"You think he is?" she asked hopefully. "He isn't truly enjoying it?"

"I doubt it," Helen said with more assurance than she felt.

"What do you think I should do?" Amanda asked, opening her innocent eyes wide.

"Depends."

"On what?"

"Do you want Luke to know you're in love with him?"

"You think I am in love with him?"

"It certainly appears that you are."

"But how do I know for sure?"

Helen thought for a moment, then said, "If a coach drove up right now and offered you a safe ride to Aunt Hattie in California, would you go if it meant you'd never see Luke again?"

"Not ever?"

"Not ever."

"I'd miss him terribly—

"Would you go?" Helen persisted.

Amanda appeared panicky. "Oh, dear! I don't know. I want to be with Aunt Hattie. I need to make my family's dream of reaching the West Coast a reality. Yet to give up a dear friend and never see him again. . ." She bit her lip. "Oh, Helen, this is silly! It isn't going to happen, so why must I fret over it?"

Helen smiled knowingly. "You don't have to fret over it. We got our answer, didn't we?"

Amanda frowned. "Perhaps I do love him, but it isn't fair of him to use Ruby to flush me out. I'm not going to fall for his trap. I'll simply pretend it doesn't bother me in the least."

"Good idea," Helen laughed. "You do that, honey. Let's see what a good actress you'd make. It will be fun to watch, but I think you're making a big mistake. If I were you—and I truly wish I had such a problem—I'd let him know how I felt and live happily ever after!"

"I couldn't be so bold. Besides, I won't be used as a pawn."

"But," Helen interjected, "what if we're wrong, and he isn't just using Ruby? Perhaps she's using him. She's a fortune hunter if I ever saw one. She flirts with Robert, too. I often wonder what made her decide to go with Luke instead of to California with the other girls. Maybe she fancies being a rancher's wife. I wouldn't trust Ruby one bit."

"So you think I should throw myself at Luke to protect him from Ruby?" Amanda asked in amazement.

"Why not?"

"I couldn't. It isn't me. If Luke cares for me, then he'll pursue me. If he wants Ruby, then that's what he gets."

"Good thing Luke didn't feel that way when Charles proposed to you. You'd be buried back there with Charles and Bella," Helen said impulsively.

Amanda gasped. "Helen!"

"I apologize. That was crude! You're right, just ignore them both. There will be plenty of men to choose from in California. Rich ones, too!"

"But not like Luke," she said wistfully, turning to look at him just as Ruby smiled up at him, flirtingly batting her long lashes. Amanda noticed Luke's face blush as he smiled back and laughed at something she said.

Amanda kicked her horse ahead to ride beside Robert for a moment. "When will we reach the ranch?" she asked.

"A few days. Getting saddle sore?" he asked.

"Sore, yes. But it has nothing to do with my saddle!" she

remarked before kicking her horse back to where Helen rode

Amanda was amazed at how skillful the men were at providing food throughout the journey. Every night they had fresh meat, fish, or fowl. Tonight they'd speared several large trout.

When the fish was cooked and plates filled, Amanda did something she'd never thought possible. She boldly squeezed between Ruby and Luke just as they were sitting down with their plates.

Luke immediately moved over to make room for her. "Hey! What a surprise!" His eyes gleamed mischievously, "I'm so glad you decided to join me." He put his arm around her shoulders lightly, in the gesture of a friendly hug. "I never get to spend any time with my little friend anymore."

"That's because you're such a busy man," Amanda remarked, looking in Ruby's direction.

"I'm never too busy for my *friends*," he said, promptly emphasizing the last word.

"That must be very difficult," she said pointedly, "since you have so many of them."

His eyes sparkled with challenge. He started to reply, then simply smiled, as if admitting defeat. The others joined them, and the conversation turned to the trail, the horses, and the ranch.

The next day it was Robert's turn to ride behind the group, so Amanda didn't have to wedge herself between Ruby and Luke, but rode beside Helen as usual.

"You said you couldn't do it!" Helen exclaimed.

"Oh, you noticed," Amanda said simply.

"I'm proud of you." Helen beamed. "You missed the best part You should have seen Ruby's face! Especially when you nearly knocked her over to sit beside Luke! I loved it!"

"You don't think I'm being cruel to Ruby?"

"No, you're just protecting what belongs to you."

Amanda smiled. "I like the sound of that!"

When they stopped to rest at noon, Luke walked by just as Ruby was dismounting. Helen and Amanda watched as Ruby judged the distance between her and Luke, then slipped just as Luke came close enough to catch her.

"Oh, my ankle!" she cried.

"Here, let me help you over to that log," Luke offered.

Helen and Amanda watched as Luke removed her shoe and examined her ankle.

"Why that no-good—"

"Helen, you promised to stop swearing," Amanda reminded her.

"*Snake!* That's the word I was going to say. Anything wrong with that?" Helen asked.

"No. It fits perfectly," Amanda agreed.

Luke shook his head. "I don't see any swelling, Ruby. Why don't you just rest it for a while."

"But it hurts terribly." She fluttered her eyelashes at him boldly. "If you hadn't caught me—"

"Stay here," Luke said, "I'll bring back some water."

"Watch this," Helen whispered.

When Luke appeared with Ruby's cup of water, Helen cried loudly, "Snake!" and pointed to where Ruby sat.

Ruby not only jumped up and ran smoothly, but shrieked like an attacking Indian. Amanda had to turn her face so no one would see her laughing.

Luke frowned at Helen and Amanda. "That wasn't necessary," he scolded, "I can tell when an ankle is injured and when it isn't." Luke turned and walked to where his brothers stood, puzzled by the scene.

Helen and Amanda appeared apologetic, but Ruby's eyes

burned with anger. "I'll get you both for this," she threatened. "Just see if I don't."

Amanda didn't have to wedge herself between Ruby and Luke at supper, for Ruby, too embarrassed to face Luke, ate with Robert. Amanda didn't dare confront Luke, for his look was unapproachable. Instead she carried her plate to a lovely cottonwood tree and prepared to eat alone, but Jared followed close behind and quickly settled comfortably beside her.

"Never saw Luke so angry," Jared commented.

"You heard what happened?" she asked.

"Helen finally told me." Jared laughed. "Don't worry, he'll get over it."

"Does he care so much for Ruby's feelings? Is that why he's so angry?"

"I doubt it. More likely it's his feelings that are hurt."

"But why?"

"He knew Ruby was faking, but what could he do? By uncovering Ruby's scheme you also bared Luke's ego."

"You mean he enjoyed Ruby's attention?"

"I don't think that so much as what Ruby's flirting brought out of you." Jared chuckled. "He loved your response, and if Ruby stops throwing herself at him, as he fears she may after that snake trick, then he'll miss your concern."

"You think I should have hidden my feelings?" Amanda asked earnestly.

"No, I don't. Honesty is always best. If that's how you feel, you should show it. You also should know we're all pulling for you. Don't disappoint us. We were proud of you last night." Jared stood, "Keep up the good work; and don't worry, he'll get over his pouting." He turned to leave but called over his shoulder, "I knew you had fire!"

*   *   *

Amanda searched the breakfast group for Luke, then nudged Helen. "Where's Luke?"

Helen gazed around the camp. "I don't know, I haven't seen him since last night."

Amanda again scanned the assembled group: Aaron, Robert, Jared, Jack, herself, and Helen. "Where's Ruby?"

"Good gracious!" exclaimed Helen. "Is she off with Luke again? That snake!"

Amanda stamped her foot. "Two snakes, I'm beginning to think!"

She walked up to Jared. "Good morning, Jared. I need to talk to Luke for a second. Know where he is?" She tried to sound nonchalant.

"He didn't tell you?" Jared shrugged. "Guess he was angrier than I thought. We're only a day's travel from home, so Luke rode ahead to prepare Mom for us. He wanted to tell her about Celia before we arrived, so she could collect herself."

"I see," Amanda said. About to ask Ruby's whereabouts, Amanda spotted her standing by the horse corral. For a moment she'd feared Luke had taken Ruby with him.

"So," Jared was saying, "if all goes well, we could be sleeping in our own beds tonight." He donned his hat. "You gals ready to go?"

Robert appeared with their horses and helped the girls mount.

Amanda truly hoped they'd reach the ranch tonight. She felt as though she'd been traveling forever. She nudged her horse closer to Helen. "What will you do when we get to the ranch?" Amanda asked.

"I don't know. I've never done anything other than—"

"Do you have family anywhere?"

111

"None that would acknowledge me. What about you, Amanda. Still planning on going to California?"

"I've thought about it and have made a decision. If Luke asks me to marry him, I'll accept and stay in Texas." She smiled warmly at Helen. "Thanks to your imaginary coach going to the coast, I realized I couldn't leave Luke—if he wants me, that is."

Helen winked. "Promise me you'll encourage him a little. I think he's crazy about you but is unsure of your feelings for him. Promise?"

"I'll try," she said. "Hush, now. Ruby's riding toward us. Let's try to be pleasant."

They both smiled as Ruby approached with a sinister look upon her face.

"I didn't think your trick was funny, yesterday," she sneered, looking directly at Amanda. She squinted when she spoke, and her lips were tight with anger. Her beauty had vanished. Amanda felt a chill run up her spine.

"If either of you knew me," she lashed out, "you would have known better than to cross me and make a fool out of me. No one ever has yet—and gotten away with it." She turned to Helen. "I said I'd get even, and I will. Soon." The lid over one of her half-closed eyes pulsated menacingly. "Very soon." She slipped her glove from one hand and drew out a large hat pin, which she quickly drove into the hindquarter of Amanda's horse. While Amanda's horse reared with a snort, Ruby drove the pin into Helen's horse.

Amanda didn't panic immediately. She fought to gain control of the horse, which she thought she could do, being an expert rider. But when Helen's horse reared and pawed the air, he caught Amanda's horse's head. Immediately her horse whinnied, shook its head, and bucked forward. He raced through the fields, despite Amanda's best efforts. The scenery flew by rapidly and holding on was about all she could manage. She heard shouts behind her and knew the men were trying to rescue her.

Holding on helplessly, Amanda watched the countryside fly by. The frantic horse jumped over a small creek, dodged trees, and trampled brush blindly, while she sat frozen with fright. Suddenly she knew they'd come to the end of their reckless ride. The horse was headed for a canyon area strewn with rocks of all sizes. The first one they hit sent Amanda flying one way, the horse the other. As she arced through the air Amanda prayed and even thought about which part of her body she should try to land on. Then everything was lost in darkness.

12

*A*manda's first view of the ranch was the ceiling in the guest room, though it took her several days to realize it.

When she first opened her eyes, she closed them again quickly, for bright sunlight flooded the room. Slowly she became accustomed to the light, and her first thought was that she was back in her own room in Ohio.

"Mama?" she heard herself whisper. "Mama?" she ventured more loudly. Soft footsteps from a distance came nearer. She tried turning her head, but sharp pain halted her. "Mama?" she asked.

Warm, soft lips kissed her cheek and forehead. She smiled. *Mama!* Mama took her hand and held it gently, caressing it lovingly. Amanda felt safe in Mama's presence and relaxed into darkness once more.

When Amanda opened her eyes again the room was dark, and she became frightened. "Mama?" her call was only slightly louder than a whisper.

The footsteps weren't so far away this time and reached her side quickly.

"Mama?" she heard her voice choke in fear.

"I'm here," Mama whispered, smoothing her forehead.

"I—I— My head hurts . . . ," she groaned.

"You'll feel better tomorrow," Mama whispered.

"You'll stay with me?" she asked, groping for the loving hand.

"I'll stay right here," Mama assured her, squeezing her hand gently.

Amanda relaxed into peaceful slumber.

Whispering voices drew Amanda from her darkness. Her head hurt, so she didn't open her eyes, but listened. Was that Phillip or Pa?

"Didn't Doc say she'd be all right? Didn't he say she'd wake up soon?"

Mama told him, "She's been awake twice. Don't worry. She'll be fine."

Phillip sounded worried. Amanda tried to open her eyes to reassure him, but again the sunlight blinded her. She shut them quickly. Amanda tried opening them several more times. By the time she succeeded, Phillip was gone. But Mama had kept her promise. Amanda still clung to her hand. She felt less panicky and lay gazing at the ceiling. Slowly memories began peeking into her consciousness. She frowned.

The wagon train kept poking into her memory, then the graves. She snapped her eyes shut. Her family was dead. *Luke!* She remembered Luke. Helen's face popped into her mind. Then she remembered Ruby sticking her horse with the pin and the reckless ride.

Whose hand was she holding! Who had so lovingly played Mama for her? Where was she?

Opening her eyes slowing and turning her head just slightly, she could see strange flowered wallpaper, white flouncy curtains, and a wooden door painted white. She couldn't make her head turn enough to see who sat beside her, holding her hand.

"Hello?" she whispered, confused as to how to address this person. "Who are you? Where am I?" she asked.

The comforting hand left hers, and the woman walked to the foot of the bed, directly in Amanda's view. Sparkling eyes smiled in her middle-aged face, and Amanda liked this woman immediately. Her dark, braided hair was wrapped about her head like a crown, flattering her eyes and golden skin.

Returning the smile, Amanda wondered who this gentle Spanish lady could be. Why had she treated her so lovingly?

With eyes still beaming, the lady spoke, "I'm Margaret Sterling, and you are an honored guest in our home. My son Luke has told me all about you."

Everything about this woman was gentle. At first Amanda thought she must be in heaven, and this was the biblical Mary.

"Then that was Luke's voice I heard?" she asked.

She nodded. "He has been here many times and is extremely concerned."

"What is wrong with me? My head hurts terribly."

"Doc Hawley examined you shortly after the boys brought you home. He diagnosed a concussion, a sprained ankle, and fractured wrist." She smiled brightly. "It sounds horrible but actually is minor, considering how serious it might have been."

Amanda's mind fled back to that day, and she gasped suddenly. "Helen! Is Helen all right?"

"Helen is fine. She wasn't injured at all. From her account

of the story, her horse kicked yours. She was able to bring hers under control."

"Did she say why our horses panicked?" Amanda asked.

"Explicitly," Margaret said, a blush accompanying her slight grimace.

Amanda started to laugh, but the pain in her head halted her. Margaret rushed to her side.

"Are you all right, dear?"

"Yes. I'm fine," she answered. "I did want to apologize for Helen's language. She's just found God, and her past—"

Margaret patted her hand affectionately. "I know. Luke explained everything. Actually, I'm very fond of Helen. She'll make a fine lady—with our help."

Amanda smiled. Her eyes felt heavy and kept closing.

"Get some sleep, Amanda," Margaret whispered, moving toward the door. "I'll leave you for a while, but if you need me, just call."

"Can I ask you something first?" Amanda said, her voice slurred with sleepiness. "Why did you pretend to be my mother last night?"

Beneath heavy lids, Amanda could see Margaret's eyes twinkle as she smiled and said simply, "I never pretend." She spun around and was gone.

Amanda next awoke to the rattle of china. The room was dimmer, so her eyes adjusted easily. She smiled, in spite of her pain. At the foot of her bed stood Luke, holding a tray. Despite his wide grin, his eyes were filled with concern. Amanda's heart thumped at seeing him and felt warmed by his caring look.

Her smile in return and perhaps some twinkling still left in her eyes arrested his apparent worry. He sighed. "You certainly know how to make a grand entrance! Welcome to the ranch."

"Thank you. Your mother is lovely."

"As untimely as your grand entrance was, it was a blessing for Mother."

"A nuisance, you mean."

"No. A blessing. You see, she'd just been told about Celia. Mother accepted God's will yet suffered extreme depression. She'd built her hopes on Celia's riding in with us. Not only did your accident take her mind from her own grief and pain, it gave her someone to fuss over."

Amanda wanted to tell Luke how Margaret mothered her but stopped herself. Something warned her to keep silent. Perhaps the situation had too many implications.

"She is a loving lady. Spanish?"

"Half. Her mother was Isabella Dela Rosa Cordella." At her blank look, he laughed and explained. "An extremely prominent family, of which I am very proud."

"And her father?" Amanda asked.

"Theodore Randall, a second cousin of Sam Houston."

"I've certainly heard of him. I'm impressed. What about your father?"

Luke grinned. "A cowboy from Kansas named Stewart Orin Sterling."

Amanda smiled. "There must be a story to go with that!"

"Oh, there is, but if I tell it, Mother will have my head on a platter! Don't worry, there's no way you'll get out of hearing every detail."

He nodded to the tray. "Will you have tea with me, so I can put down this awkward tray?"

She nodded with a smile.

He set the tray on a nearby table and righted the turned-over china cups in their saucers.

"But Luke, there are three cups," she observed.

He turned with a mischievous grin. "Someone wants to join us, if you're up to it?"

"Who? Helen?" she asked anxiously.

"No. Dad. He can't wait to meet you—unless you don't feel well enough. I can tell him you'll see him tomorrow. . . ."

Amanda couldn't imagine why his father would be so anxious to meet her but was flattered enough to agree.

"Be right back," he said, hurrying to the door.

Amanda hoped the surprise she felt didn't surface in her face when Stewart Sterling filled the doorway, moments later. She never expected Luke's father to look as he did. Standing about six foot three, he towered over Luke, who had always seemed so tall to her. His body reminded Amanda of a Greek statue, with a large, muscular chest and small waist held up by long, lanky, slightly bowed legs. He cut a magnificent figure, with hair lighter blond than even Celia's had been. He had the same bushy eyebrows as Luke and Jared, except his were yellow and, like his hair, slightly streaked with white. Stewart Sterling's face appeared rosy, and the smile included his bright-blue eyes.

"So this is Amanda!" His melodic, low, powerful voice filled the small room. "Sorry to barge in so soon, but after the introduction Luke gave—Well, I couldn't wait to make your acquaintance. Welcome to our home."

His presence filled the room so completely that Amanda was at a loss for words. Finally she managed a small "Thank you."

He sat lightly, for a man his size, on a chair Luke provided.

Luke poured tea and handed them each a cup.

Looking at his father, Luke smiled and said, "Well, can we keep her?"

Mr. Sterling's booming laughter nearly startled Amanda. She'd have to get used to this huge, loud, yet gentle man. She blushed at Luke's remark.

Seeing her color, Stewart explained, "This is a long-running family joke. Luke always brought home something he begged to keep. Let's see." He scratched his chin as Luke often did while thinking. "Once it was a black-and-white kitten, another time a stray dog that had only three legs, and we'll never forget the Indian boy!"

"Indian boy?" Amanda asked in wonder.

"Yep." Stewart laughed. "Luke found him in the woods. The boy was about twelve, spoke no English, and Luke wanted to keep him. That was the only one we made him return!"

Amanda smiled. Luke had a delightful family. She loved them all.

They chatted casually for some time before Stewart and Luke stood to leave. Walking toward the door, Stewart turned and smiled at her, then winked at Luke. "Well, Son, I guess we'll keep this one."

"Come in," Amanda responded to the light tap on her bedroom door the next morning.

Helen's red head peeked into the bright room. "You accepting visitors?" she asked.

"Helen!" Amanda cried. "Oh, I'm so glad to see you!" She opened her arms to enfold her friend.

Helen hesitated initially to enter Amanda's warm embrace, then returned it lovingly, as if the gesture were foreign to her but welcome.

"You gave us all a pretty scare, I'll tell ya!" she exclaimed, sitting at the foot of the bed.

"Tell me everything that happened from the moment the horse threw me." Amanda sat up straight, with wide eyes, and folded her hands. "Don't leave out one detail."

Helen laughed. "Guess that bump on the head didn't hurt you none. Same old Amanda!"

"Do begin the story! I'm on pins and needles!"

Smoothing Amanda's coverlet, Helen began, "You recall

that sword Ruby drove into your horse's rump, don't you?"

Amanda laughed, "Helen! That was a hat pin!"

"Could have fooled my horse!" She grinned. "Anyhow, my horse kicked yours, but I was able to control mine. Not soon enough though, to help you. The men took off after you, but your horse ran like lightning! The men found you only moments after you were thrown. In fact, Aaron claims he saw you hit the ground."

Helen shook her flaming curls, "Never realized how much those fellows cared for you until then. You could have been their own sister the way they fussed and worried."

Tears burned Amanda's eyes. It felt as if she had a family again. Knowing she'd soon be in tears, she changed the subject quickly: "What happened to Ruby? Is she here? How did the men deal with her and what she'd done?"

"I'm ashamed to say I almost pulled every hair from her head, and the men had to pull me off her. I thought she'd killed you, and I saw red! Can't ever recall being so angry! Robert said he hadn't heard such language since the last time he'd visited the London waterfront.

"Jared," Helen continued, "took Ruby aside, once they had made you comfortable and ready to travel, and talked to her. I don't know what they said, but she cried, and he seemed kind yet firm. They made a stretcher for you from horse blankets and tree limbs and dragged you behind their horses, which slowed us considerably and brought Luke out looking for us."

Helen chuckled and shook her head as if recalling a loving memory. "When he saw the stretcher. . . . Well, I never saw anyone so alarmed! We were only a few hours' travel from the ranch when he met us, but the rest of the trip you rode in royal style!"

Amanda cocked her head, "What do you mean?"

"I mean Luke Sterling immediately picked you up from

the dusty stretcher and had you placed in front of him on his horse. He rode all the way home with you—like a baby in his arms." Helen smiled in fond remembrance. "He talked to you the whole time, too, but I couldn't hear what he said. Soft, crooning things."

"Oh, Helen!" Amanda whispered, tears streaming down her cheeks. "You make it sound so—so—"

"Romantic?" Helen put in.

She nodded.

Helen continued, "That isn't all. Wait until you hear the rest! Ruby was terribly quiet the whole time. She rode alone and spoke to no one. Luke ignored her completely until you were tucked into bed safely and the doctor was examining you. Then he summoned her into the study, and—" She whispered secretly, "I wasn't eavesdropping, mind you, just happened to be passing by, you understand."

Amanda smiled knowingly. "Go on, Helen!"

"He asked her to leave the ranch!"

"But where did he expect her to go?"

She shrugged. "I didn't hear the whole conversation, but the next thing I knew, Aaron was escorting her off the premises."

"Where did he take her?" Amanda asked, eyes wide.

"The nearest town, Laredo. According to Jared, she found a job right away in a saloon."

"Poor Ruby," sighed Amanda.

"You serious?" asked Helen.

"I am. I've discovered that people with different backgrounds acquire different slants on life—like yourself, for instance. Not everyone is blessed with a loving, God-fearing, Bible-reading family like Luke's or my own. I suppose the more difficult the background the harder the crust around that heart."

"But," Helen reminded her, "it was that very emptiness

that lead me to accept God in my life. I've never felt loved before. You'd think Ruby would be as hungry for God as I was."

"Her misfortunes may have been different," Amanda said thoughtfully. "She may have been loved her whole life, but by the wrong type of people. Evidently her need isn't love. If only we knew where she was vulnerable, we could aim for it and help her."

"Ruby's beyond help," Helen protested disgustedly.

"No, Helen. No one is beyond help."

"But Jared told me he tried for hours to help her, and she plain refused to have anything to do with religion or God."

"If we get another opportunity, we'll try again," said Amanda, "and pray for her."

"I guess," Helen said slowly, with downcast eyes, "I have a long way to go—I mean with God. I'm trying, but some things are still difficult for me."

"Me, too!" Amanda smiled. "I gave Him up completely and am so ashamed."

"And I thought thrashing Ruby was the right thing to do, after what she did. Figured God would allow it, seeing as you're one of His and all!"

Amanda threw her head back in laughter, until her pain forced her to stop. "Oh, Helen! I'm so glad I have you here!"

Helen sobered. "Yes, but not for long, I'm afraid."

"What do you mean?"

"I can't stay and sponge off these swell people. I have to find a job and—"

"Hush!" Amanda scolded. "We'll think of something. Together we'll figure out what to do. You can travel to California with me!" she suggested excitedly.

13

While Helen's visit had cheered Amanda, it had also given her much to ponder. Her goal of reaching California and Aunt Hattie seemed to diminish more as her feelings for Luke grew. What should she do?

She tossed restlessly, then wished she hadn't, for now her bed was crumpled and sloppy. It would be just like Luke to pop in and see her like this. Yet she continued to toss about, trying to find a solution and a cool position that didn't cause pain.

Amanda tried to envision Luke cradling her upon his horse; tears streamed down her cheeks. She punched her pillow. He cared! She cared, too! How could she leave? By then she was sniffling and wiping tears and didn't hear footsteps approach until a loving hand caressed her shoulder. Amanda looked up into the soft eyes of Margaret Sterling. The gentle lady wiped Amanda's tears with a white lace handkerchief, which felt as soft as her touch.

Patting Amanda's hand, Margaret sat down on the side

of the bed. Studying Amanda's face carefully, she whispered, "I'm surprised to find you weeping. I thought we'd made you happy and at home here. Did we do something wrong?"

"Oh, no!" Amanda's voice croaked, and tears of a different nature rolled down her cheeks again. She shook her head. "You've all been perfect. It's— it's—" Amanda felt at a loss to explain what troubled her, for she wasn't sure herself.

"Were you missing your family?"

"No!" Amanda exclaimed quickly, then, "well, yes, but not then. . . . I mean. . . ." She cast her eyes downward, hunting for the right explanation.

"Did Helen upset you, then?" Mrs. Sterling asked with concern-filled eyes.

"Yes," Amanda blurted. Quickly she retreated with, "No, not really, she just—" Amanda began to cry in earnest. Her emotions could no longer be held in check, especially with Margaret's sympathy touching her deeply.

Luke's mother took Amanda into her arms, cradling her as she wept. "Cry all you can, dear," she soothed, rocking her lovingly, "it's long overdo. You've been through so much!"

When Amanda lay spent in Margaret's arms, the gentle mother spoke softly. "Amanda, I want you to know you can talk to me about anything, as if you were. . . ." She hesitated then added positively, "As if you were my own daughter."

Amanda looked up at her and smiled.

"I mean it. If something is troubling you, perhaps I can help. Celia was very much like you."

"How do you know what I'm like?" Amanda asked with a sniffle.

"I know. You're sensitive, loving, gentle, with a touch of

stubborn pride. You were reared as a lady, yet inside you want to act differently sometimes, but cannot. I also think you are either in love and don't know it or know it and don't want to be." Margaret looked down at her and smiled. "How did I score?"

Amanda sat up in amazement. "But how could you possibly know all that?"

Luke's mother smiled knowingly, "I was your age once, and mothered four daughters, so I've had a little practice. But mostly, Amanda, it's because you remind me so strongly of Celia. Maybe that's why—" She stopped and smiled. "Tell me the specifics. Just because I'm Luke's mother doesn't mean I can't be trusted with your secrets. We women stick together."

"It's not that I don't trust you," Amanda answered quickly. "But because I truly don't know what I feel or what I want that I hesitate to discuss it."

Margaret smiled with understanding. "Tell me what you know so far. Maybe I can help."

Amanda looked at the dark, beautiful woman. She still looked the part of the biblical Mary to Amanda, with her dark salt-and-pepper hair pulled back gently into a bun at the nape of her neck and her soft brown eyes and slender, graceful body movements. Amanda sighed. This woman was so easy to talk to, and she trusted her.

Amanda took a deep breath before unburdening her heavy heart. "I do love Luke, but I'm not sure I know the difference between love and friendship love."

"Why should there be a difference?" Margaret asked. "Mr. Sterling is my best friend, and I love him dearly."

"But I don't feel for Luke what I felt for a young, handsome man on the train. He wasn't half the man Luke is, mind you. Yet whenever he smiled or touched me, I got goose bumps and felt flushed and giddy."

"And," Mrs. Sterling asked, "what do you feel around Luke?"

Amanda smiled. "Around Luke I feel many things. The most noticeable is a warmth here," she touched her chest. "I feel safe, secure, comfortable, and.   ." Amanda stopped and blushed.

"And what?" Margaret prompted.

"When Luke holds me in his arms, I feel . . . ," she searched for the right words. "I feel . . . like that's the only place in the world I ever want to be. Sometimes I crave to be hugged and held by him, just so I can feel that."

"And his kisses?" Margaret asked without embarrassment.

Amanda blushed. "I've only had two. Bells didn't ring, and I didn't feel faint." She smiled, remembering. "But it felt as if I'd been kissing him like that forever, instead of the first and second time." Amanda looked at Luke's mother hesitantly. "There's something else I feel, but it's almost too strange to mention, and I'm not sure the words available can possibly describe it."

"Try. So far I can relate to everything you're feeling."

"All right." Amanda pressed her lips together, gazed at the ceiling, and thought carefully how to word her unusual sensation. "Sometimes when I'm with Luke—especially the times we were close—I wanted to . . . to . . merge my soul with his, to become one. It's difficult to explain.   "

With tear-filled eyes, Mrs. Sterling said sincerely, "Amanda, I can't tell you that you are in love with my son; that's one of those things you must decide for yourself. But let me ask you a question. Why do you think you should feel goose bumps and feel faint? Who ever told you that was love?"

"I . . . don't know. I guess from books and poems I've read. What was it, then, that I felt for the man on the trail?

It frightened me, because he wasn't the type of man I'd want to spend my life with. In fact he turned out to be quite despicable. So why did I react to him so strongly?"

"Hm-m-m, he was handsome, you said?" she asked thoughtfully.

"Oh, yes! And terribly charming."

"Oh! You mean the ah-h . . . gambler that . . . um . . . coerced our Celia? Luke told me about him."

"Yes."

Margaret smiled knowingly. "That man was a professional. He had his act honed to perfection. You and Celia reacted just as any normal, well-reared, inexperienced young ladies would, which is why he was so successful. What you experienced was a thrilling adventure or infatuation. I'm glad you feel more than mere goose bumps for Luke. I certainly wouldn't marry someone *just* because he gave me goose bumps."

Margaret's tone took on a reminiscent quality. "I remember having similar feelings when I met Mr. Sterling. It was such a romantic adventure! I did feel a few goose bumps, but they soon faded and were replaced by a permanent condition called love.

"As you know, I was a rich rancher's pampered only daughter. I was given whatever my heart desired. It became boring, and every man I knew was too attentive. I couldn't tell if he was attracted to me or my father's wealth. So when my father's cousins in Kansas invited me for a summer visit, I was ready for a diversion—and some fun!"

Amanda smiled and made herself comfortable. "Is this the story Luke promised you'd tell? He wouldn't tell me. Said you'd have his head if he did!"

Margaret laughed softly. "They all know I love to tell it. The best adventure of my life!"

"As soon as my chaperon, Tia, and I were in the stage-

coach I unveiled my plan. As enthusiastic as I, she agreed."
Touching Amanda's hand, she explained. "Now, you must
understand the situation. Tia was a mere five years older
than I. Her mother had been my maid and chaperon all my
life, but was not well, so they sent Tia. Tia and I had grown
up together, and she was a lovely girl. I decided we'd switch
roles. She would be Margarita Cordella Randall, and I the
chaperon-maid, Tia. Having seen her many times holding
my dresses before her in the looking glass and prancing
about acting like me when she thought no one saw, I knew
she'd be thrilled with the role. She played it well, too."

Amanda shook her head. "Didn't your relatives know
the difference?"

"Oh, no," Mrs. Sterling explained. "We'd never met.
Dad had visited them several times when in the area on
business, but they had never seen me. It was perfect

"It worked, but almost backfired, as dishonesty usually
does."

Amanda drew up her knees and hugged them. "Please
continue, I can't wait to hear the story."

"Everything went well. No one suspected. We were the
same size, so we simply switched clothing and roles. It also
made me aware of all the work poor Tia had to do and how
difficult the job could be at times. I had to unpack her
clothes, iron them—I must admit I burned a hole in my best
morning dress." She shook her head in fond remembrance.
"It was the adventure of my life!"

"I had to eat in the kitchen with the other hired help and
sleep in a small room off the cowboy's bunkhouse with four
other maids. But," she smiled, with sparkling eyes, "that's
how I met Mr. Sterling. He was magnificent!"

"He never would have approached me as myself, but as
a maid, I was of his class. It was probably the adventure and
the mischievous role that gave me the goose bumps when

he first touched me. I felt thrilled and frightened all at once. He was a gentleman though, and I soon discovered I had nothing to fear by meeting him to watch the prairie sunsets."

Eyes shiny with emotion and remembrance, Margaret said abruptly, "Without boring you with the details, we fell in love. If you think that was all, and we then lived happily ever after, it wasn't that easy! I fell into the tangled web I'd woven and didn't know how to get out of it. He loved me, thinking me a person whom I was not. I'd never thought of whether or not he'd love me as Margarita Randall, wealthy rancher's daughter. I was terrified to tell him the truth."

She hesitated, and Amanda burst out, "What did you do?"

"I did nothing. I couldn't. I feared losing him. I kept putting off doing what I knew I had to do. Then our farce was discovered, and everyone knew the truth.

"Father's cousin decided to throw a party for their guest, and the most prominent people in the vicinity were invited. Unknown to me, one of them happened to be a priest from the mission near our ranch, who had been sent to Topeka for further schooling. He'd stopped on his way and been invited to the gathering. Father Raphael had been a family friend since before I was born. He immediately demanded to know where Margarita was. When they pointed to Tia in confusion, he adamantly insisted she was an impostor.

"That's when I decided to come forward. What a mass of confusion! The whole ranch had wind of it in an hour. My only thoughts that night as I lay in bed looking at the stars were for Stewart Sterling and how he'd react to the news.

"The next day I searched for him. He was nowhere to be found. He'd left the ranch in anger, so the others said. I was heartbroken.

"He returned the next day, and I finally confronted him.

He refused to look at me. I'd never seen him so angry. He said hurtful things to me, but I begged him to hear my side of the story. He did, and I had to do a lot of fast talking and explaining. Though he softened, he refused to return to Texas with me and meet my family. Since he wouldn't allow me to stay in Kansas with him, I tearfully asked just what his plans for me were. He said he needed time to think. Three days later, as they prepared to drive Tia and me to the stagecoach, he finally approached me with an answer.

"He said he still loved me and wanted to spend his life with me but would not until my father gave his permission. He said he'd wait one month, then pay a visit to our ranch and ask for my hand.

"I worried all the way home. How could I get Father's permission to marry a cowboy?" Margaret smiled. "But I did. It took nearly the whole month and much begging, crying, and going without food. Like always, I got what I wanted, but for the last time, for Mr. Sterling unspoiled me Reading the Bible aloud nightly, he showed me how God loves marriage and how he wanted marriages to be set up Mr. Sterling has always been the head of our home and our spiritual leader. He loved me as the Bible said he should, and because he loved me, he treated me wonderfully. So wonderfully, that the part the Bible gave me was easy. It isn't difficult to honor and obey a man who loves you as Christ loves His church. I don't remember my parents being as happy and as in love as we are. I know our love and marriage have lasted and been blessed because we made it a threesome instead of a twosome: God and Mr. and Mrs Sterling. We've been truly blessed."

"I can feel the love and specialness here,' Amanda said

'Mr. Sterling is a wonderful man. My adventure was wrong and dishonest, but something good did come out of it." Margaret stood and began to straighten and smooth Amanda's bed.

"You know, Mr. Sterling would not take a penny from my father. He worked hard on the ranch and earned everything given us. I was never so proud of anyone. In a short time my parents loved him as I did. When they died five years later, we inherited everything, which Mr. Sterling felt all right to accept—for the children's sake, he said."

"What a wonderful story! No wonder you love to tell it!" said Amanda.

Margaret laughed. "But have I helped you any? The goose bumps I felt when I first met Mr. Sterling stopped when reality began. I think the excitement of the adventure was half of it. Then, when I thought I'd never see him again, I felt panicky and knew I couldn't live without him. When he finally arrived in Texas, I was never so glad to see anyone! That's when I felt the warm glow and the feeling of wanting to become one with him. That isn't strange, Amanda; in fact, it's even scriptural." She pointed to an embroidered oval hanging on the far wall. "You can't read it from here. Let me bring it over." She crossed the room and brought the framed cloth to Amanda. "Here, read it aloud."

"For we are members of his body, of his flesh, and of his bones," Amanda read. "For this cause shall a man leave his father and mother, and shall be joined unto his wife, and they two shall be one flesh. Ephesians five, verses thirty and thirty-one."

She handed it back, "It's beautiful."

"It was a wedding gift from my mother. She made it herself."

Margaret replaced the verse to its place upon the far wall. She returned and sat beside Amanda and rubbed her hand. "Do you feel any better?"

"I am still confused about whether or not I should go to California. I wanted to make my family's dream come true, but my feelings for Luke have mixed up my priorities. I even told Helen just before my accident that if Luke asked me to stay, I would. But he hasn't asked, and I'm having some second thoughts."

"Pray about it," Mrs. Sterling said as she walked to the door. "Then do what your heart leads you to do "

14

Margaret Sterling had surprised Amanda the next morning by dressing her in a lovely green dress that matched her eyes and having Luke carry her down to a courtyard for breakfast with the family.

Stewart Sterling towered over the head of the table while lovely Margaret graced the opposite end. Though the dining was informal and on the patio overlooking the vast meadows of the ranch, the couple gave the table class. Amanda was placed beside Stewart with Luke across from her. Aaron, Jared, and Robert were there and joked and teased her about her runaway horse and her grand entrance to the ranch.

Since Edward, Emily, and Sarah were married with families of their own, they were not present. She did, however, finally meet Elvira, a pleasant, down-to-earth person, whom Amanda liked immediately.

After Mr. Sterling said grace, they were served breakfast by a maid everyone called Annie, a thick-set Mexican lady who walked heavily and handled the food and dishes roughly but efficiently. Annie spoke kindly yet gruffly, and Amanda thought she must have had to be tough to deal with the Sterling boys through the years.

"How does it feel to be out of bed, Amanda?" Mr. Sterling's voice dominated even the outdoors.

"It feels wonderful. It was a pleasant surprise."

"You look beautiful," said Helen, from the other end ot the table.

Amanda smiled. "Thank you, Helen. I feel much better. My headache is only slight, and my wrist and ankle aren't quite so painful either. When do you suppose I can walk?" she directed her question at Stewart for some reason and wasn't quite sure why, except that he dominated the gathering.

"That's up to Doc Hawley." He looked at his wife 'When did Hawley say he'd be back, love?"

"He said in a few days, and that was four days ago. If he doesn't come today, we'll send Luke for him."

Luke looked at his mother meaningfully. "Did you forget I'll be gone today?"

"Oh! That's right. We'll send one of the other boys."

Luke merely smiled at Amanda. She wondered where he was going and felt disappointed that she wouldn't get to spend time with him now that she was out of bed.

Margaret smiled at Amanda. "It's a lovely day. Would you enjoy staying out here in the courtyard, or would you rather Luke took you inside? You could sit in the living room, or perhaps you're tired and would like to go back to your room?"

"I'd love to stay here. I wish I could walk through your garden, it's lovely." Amanda gazed longingly at the two moon-shaped areas, bursting with flowers and shrubs, between two sections of the large, one-story house. Amanda couldn't see much of the house from where she sat, but it looked as if it were shaped like a large letter *U*. They sat in the curve of the *U*, on a brick-floored patio, looking toward the open meadows. The house was white stone, with many trellises of ivy growing profusely up its walls.

She'd seen a bit of the house inside as she was being carried downstairs. It appeared a lovely, richly furnished home.

Immediately after they'd finished eating, Luke, extremely attentive, lifted Amanda from her chair and placed her on a sofa along the coolest wall of the patio. It felt good to be close again, and she wished she could throw her arms around his neck and hug him. The only hint that he felt the same way was a slight hesitation in letting go of her, once he had her securely seated.

The others scattered to their various chores, except Helen and Margaret, who lingered at the table, talking intently.

Luke sat beside her. With sad, concern-filled eyes, he blurted, "I'm sorry for what happened. It was all my fault."

Amanda tipped her head in confusion. "What do you mean?"

"Ruby" was all he said.

"How is what *she* did *your* fault? You weren't even there."

With downcast eyes, he hesitated, looking uncomfortable. He scooped his hair from his face and squinted slightly.

Amanda smiled. *Same, lovable Luke.*

Finally, he stuttered, "I—I encouraged her behavior. It's my fault. I could have stopped her— My male ego stopped me, I guess. I'm sorry." He looked at her solemnly. "I've never been so sorry. You could have been killed. You scared me out of ten good years of my life as it is!" He smiled a little, then sobered. "Honestly, Amanda, I am sorry."

"You're forgiven." She smiled. "I hope you've forgiven Ruby, too."

"That's something I'm still working on."

"Remember what you told me about the weeds?"

He grinned and nodded. "I'm going into Laredo today. Maybe I'll stop and set things right with her."

Amanda could feel a bit of the old jealousy stab at her again. "You don't have to overdo it, you know "

Luke smiled. "You still care?"

"Of course I do. I wouldn't want my best friend involved with someone so dangerous," she said, trying to make light of her concern.

He stood. "Yes, that's right, your *friend*." He turned to leave, calling over his shoulder sarcastically, "*Adios, amiga.*"

"Luke!" she called after him.

He stopped and walked slowly back. "Yes, my *good friend*, what can I do for you?"

"Please don't leave angry. Did I say something wrong?"

He sighed and sat down beside her. Searching her eyes, he said simply, "I'm growing a bit tired of this friendship thing. Is that all I'll ever be to you?"

Amanda felt her heart pounding. *Here it is,* she thought, *a confrontation.* She couldn't hide behind friendship any longer, for he was asking, and she must answer. She recalled the answer his mother had given her and decided to use that, at least to hold him at bay temporarily.

"Why not? Your mother told me that your father is her best friend."

Luke shook his head slowly and said, "My parents happen to also be very much in love. That makes it different."

Amanda felt sympathy for Luke. She was making this difficult for him. Hadn't she promised Helen she'd encourage him? She loved Luke. Why couldn't she let him know it? Why was she afraid to commit herself?

"Luke . . . ," she began hesitantly. As he waited for her words, she could see hope in his eyes. She couldn't disappoint him!

"Luke . . . I . . . I. . . ." The words stuck in her throat.

"Amanda," he interrupted. "Helen is waiting. I'll see you at supper."

"Helen?" she asked. "Why is Helen going to Laredo?"

"She insists on getting a job."

Amanda looked at the table, where Helen and Margaret were still having a serious discussion.

"Luke, not the saloon . . . ," she said with a worried look.

"Mother is trying to lend her enough money to start a business of some sort, which is what they are discussing."

Amanda sat up straight, eyes wide.

"Luke, that's a wonderful idea! I have some money from my father. I could help."

Luke looked displeased and said, "I thought you wanted to travel to California once you've recuperated. That's another reason I'm going to Laredo. Father suggests you sail to San Francisco instead of traveling overland. I have a friend with a small ship who might give you passage, but it will cost a few hundred dollars."

Amanda closed her mouth quickly instead of blurting that she would rather stay and go into business with Helen. She wasn't sure. What did she want? Luke hadn't asked her to stay.

"What do you think I should do?" she asked.

"Oh, sail. It's much safer, and the gulf isn't far. Once you get around the cape, the rest is a breeze. No Indians, no pushing heavy wagons up mountains and across rivers."

"Would I sail alone?" she asked.

Luke hesitated and rubbed his hands together nervously. "Well, perhaps we can find someone else who is interested in going. I'll discuss it with my friend Seth Turner, who owns the ship. He may have other passengers, with the Gold Rush fever still spreading heavy in these parts." He stood. "I'll let you know."

Amanda's heart sank. He didn't show even a hint that he'd like her to stay.

Supper was served in the loveliest, most elegant dining room, and afterwards they all retired to the drawing room. Elvira played the piano while they enjoyed freshly brewed coffee

"Would you like me to carry you outside for some air?" Luke whispered. Amanda nodded without hesitation, and he lifted her effortlessly.

He sat beside her on the patio sofa.

"Did you talk to your friend Seth?" she asked anxiously.

"Yes, and the news is not good, I'm afraid."

"What do you mean?"

"He's making a trip to San Francisco, but not until after Christmas. He's transporting a large shipment, and it won't be ready until then. However," he added, "at that time there will be fifty other passengers, both men and women. So it may be well worth the wait. What do you think?"

Amanda studied him closely. His face was bland. She couldn't detect a clue from his looks as to his true feelings about her leaving.

"If your family doesn't mind me staying that long, I'll gladly wait," she answered without enthusiasm.

"Cheer up." He lifted her chin with his hand. "The time will go fast, and in no time at all you'll be safely with Aunt Hattie "

She smiled weakly. "What about Helen's business venture?"

"I probably should let her tell you the details, but it looks promising. We rented an empty store today, though she hasn't yet decided what to do with it. Mother thinks Laredo needs another good clothing store, with hats and furs. Helen is leaning toward a bakery. She wouldn't need as much money to start a bakery as she would to stock a clothing store. Mother is still trying to make her understand we'll back her up financially for as long as need be."

"That's very generous of your family," Amanda said. "What happened to the girl I knew as Louise?"

"Dad sent her to New Orleans, where she has family. Her story was much like yours and Celia's. She was a decent girl from a respectable family. Mother said she promised to write, but we haven't heard anything yet."

"Your folks enjoy helping others, don't they?" she asked.

"Yes. They always have."

"You're like them. That's why you were so anxious to help me when my family died. I can see where all your good traits come from: your helpfulness, your concern, and your godliness."

Luke smiled shyly. "Where do you suppose my bad traits come from?"

Amanda's answer was a yawn, and Luke jumped up. "You're tired. I'll take you upstairs immediately, and Mother will help you get ready for bed."

When he lifted her, she put both arms around his neck, instead of one, and rested her cheek on his. Hadn't she promised Helen she'd encourage him?

His grip on her immediately tightened. Luke turned his head slightly, and their lips touched, softly at first, then longingly.

How good it feels to be in his arms and kissed by him again, she thought. He broke the kiss and gazed into her eyes deeply, their foreheads touching. *Ask me*, she silently coached, *ask me to stay. This time I'll say yes.* He kissed her lips again lightly and planted small kisses on her cheek and down her neck, until goose bumps stood out on her arms. Goose bumps from Luke! She looked at her arm in wonder. His eyes followed.

"You're cold, I better get you inside." He hurriedly rushed her back to her room, with Margaret immediately behind to assist.

He let her down on the bed gently, and while his mother's back was turned, as she fished in the drawer for a nightgown, he kissed her lips lightly.

"Good night, Amanda," he whispered hoarsely. "I'm glad you won't be leaving for a while."

"So am I," she whispered back.

He turned and smiled before leaving the room.

Amanda felt warm all over and thrilled by her romantic encounter yet disappointed that he hadn't asked her to stay. She must think of a way to encourage him toward asking her, for now, the last thing she wanted to do was leave Luke Sterling and the SOS Ranch.

15

*A*manda hobbled about the kitchen, using her hand-carved cane, helping Annie and Margaret can and preserve for winter. It felt wonderful to be walking by herself, though she had to admit she missed Luke carrying her. She smiled as she filled her jar full of hot, steaming peppers. The Sterling household felt like home. Yesterday she'd made her first trip to church in Laredo and heard Pastor Edward Sterling give a moving message. She had met Emily and Margaret's precocious but precious grandsons, John, Raymond, and Theo. Amanda still hadn't met Sarah, because she was home awaiting the birth of their first child. Luke promised to take her for a visit as soon as the baby came. Sarah and her husband lived ten miles from Laredo, while the Sterlings only lived four miles east of the rustic town.

. The Sterling home seemed quiet now that Elvira had gone back to live in Laredo, where she had a room behind the schoolhouse. Helen had moved in behind her new bakery.

Luke was gone nearly every day, either helping Helen in Laredo or helping his father with the ranch.

While she daydreamed, Amanda toyed with the pepper-covered ladle, circling the jar rim lazily.

Margaret asked, "Is that jar ready to be covered?" When Amanda didn't answer, she asked a bit more loudly, "Amanda? Is that jar ready to be covered?"

"I'm sorry." Amanda jumped to attention. "I was thinking about yesterday. Yes, the jar is ready."

"Sundays are my favorite, too," Margaret beamed. "I get to see my grown children, my grandchildren, and hear my son preach in the same church where Mr. Sterling and I were married: I can hardly wait until Sarah's baby is born. I'm anxious to fill my home with all the grandchildren I can squeeze in!"

Amanda smiled. "You do enjoy them so much. And Joanna is such a lovely girl! When are she and Jared to be married?"

"They postponed the wedding because of Celia's death and illness in Joanna's family. They've decided to wait until spring."

"Oh, dear!" Amanda gasped. "I'll miss it, then!"

Margaret straightened her apron. "Yes, I guess you will." Amanda thought she was about to say more but bit her lip and remained silent.

Disappointment surged through Amanda. Not only was she to miss the wedding, but neither Luke nor his mother had even asked her to reconsider and stay.

As if in answer to Amanda's faded look, Margaret finally said, "We will all miss you, but think of the exciting trip you'll be taking. A trip to California by ship. It sounds wonderful! And you'll see your aunt again. I doubt Jared or Joanna would want to spoil that for you. None of us would. But you'll be with us in spirit."

Before Amanda could respond, the men burst into the room to wash for lunch, as the noon meal was served in the kitchen. Stewart Sterling bent his tall frame over the large kitchen sink and washed briskly; then drying his hands, he moved over so Jared, Aaron, and Robert could wash.

"Where's Luke?" he asked in a voice that still startled Amanda with its intensity.

"He and Jack are breaking that new stallion," Jared replied.

"Didn't they hear Annie ring the bell?" he boomed.

"Guess not," said Robert. "Annie's getting weak in her old age and probably didn't ring loud enough."

"You won't say I'm so old when you want seconds on this blueberry pie tonight!" Annie retorted as she moved toward the back door. She rang the dinner bell again, pulling on the rope with all her strength.

"Let me show you how to ring the bell," Robert laughed and pulled the rope with all his might. The heavy rope snapped, Robert fell over backwards with the remnant in his hands, and the bell gave out a slight tinkle.

"Guess you showed me! Now better fix that thing before supper, or no one will eat!" Annie scolded.

Mr. Sterling and the boys roared with laughter until a gunshot silenced the room.

"Who's hunting so close to the house?" roared Stewart.

"I'll check," Robert yelled as he flew out the door.

Amanda and Margaret helped Annie by handing her the bowls to fill with hot, steamy soup. Stewart paced by the door while Aaron and Jared rolled up their sleeves and pulled out their chairs, preparing to eat.

Everyone froze when they heard Robert racing toward the back porch, yelling, "Hurry! Pa, come quick, Luke's hurt! The horse threw him, then trampled him! Jack shot the horse!"

144

"Dear God . . . ," Stewart prayed as he raced for the corral.

Margaret, Amanda, and the boys followed. When they turned the corner of the barn, they stopped, frozen in their tracks. Amanda gasped. Could that be Luke? Margaret grasped her hand and squeezed it. Amanda squeezed hers back. They needed each other.

Amanda would have doubted that the bloody mass before her was Luke, were it not for his familiar shirt and vest. Luke's father carefully turned him over so he lay face up. Amanda and Margaret looked away with a shudder of tears. Luke's face was puddled in blood and covered with hoofprints and dust.

Stewart Sterling momentarily hesitated between breaking down and taking charge. Taking charge won, and he began shouting orders. "Jack, get a stretcher. Jared, prepare his bed. Robert, fetch Doc, fast. Aaron, help me loosen his clothing and put him on the stretcher."

He bowed his head then, and Amanda knew he prayed for his crushed and broken son.

Watching them lift Luke onto the stretcher, Amanda wondered if there was any hope. Was he alive? His body, so bloody, bruised, and broken, seemed incredibly limp and lifeless. Should she pray? Or should she simply let the Sterlings pray? Would God listen to her? To any of them? If God's will was to take Luke, could she accept that?

Margaret's hand patted then squeezed hers. She looked up at Luke's mother, who gave her a tearful smile.

"Trust in the Lord," she whispered.

How can I? How can we? Amanda cried to herself. To Margaret she said, "I'll try."

As they followed the stretcher into the house Amanda felt the urge to cry, yet could not. The strong mother beside her encouraged her. If Luke's mother could be strong, so could she. Besides, if she broke down it might upset Margaret and her brave courageousness.

Amanda wondered that the hall clock ticked so loudly. Why had she never noticed it before? She, the Sterling family, and Jack had been waiting hours in the drawing room while Doc Hawley and Stewart were in a bedroom with Luke. There had been no verdict yet, except that at the time they carried him in he was alive. Edward had arrived with Doc Hawley, but Aaron had decided not to alarm the other siblings until more news became available.

Amanda poured herself another cup of coffee and stood silently by the window, gazing idly at the vast meadows.

Jared joined her, taking her cold hand in his. "You poor kid!" he whispered compassionately. "Lost your family, and now—"

"Don't, please!" she interrupted sharply. "Don't give me sympathy!" She added more kindly, "I'll crumble." She looked up at him with tearing eyes. "What I need is strength."

"God is our refuge and strength . . . ," Edward said, joining them.

"Yes, but—"

"You're remembering the last time you asked God for a life, aren't you?" he asked. "Luke told me everything." She nodded sadly.

"I thought you had gotten over that when you found out what future your family would have had, had they lived."

"I did, but my fear has returned. I know that God will do what's best for Luke, because Luke lives for Him, but it's still difficult to accept."

"It always will be for us, because we are human. Even Jesus was sad to hear his friend Lazarus had died—not because He would never see him again, but because He'd miss Lazarus here on earth. Remember how Lazarus's sisters carried on when he died?" He looked at her and smiled, "Jesus was deeply moved because of the sorrow that sickness and death brought. The Bible says, 'Jesus wept.' Just continue praying and asking for strength. Luke belongs to God. God has the right to claim him whenever He chooses. Death is not the worst thing that can happen to Luke." Edward put his arm around Amanda gently. "I'd grieve more if Luke were falling away from God and into the world of sin. That, in my opinion, is real dying."

"This is the most wonderful family I've ever known." Amanda sniffled. "How you can minister to me, when your own flesh and blood is perhaps dying, I'll never know. This whole family is so strong, good, and unselfish." She looked up at Edward and smiled. "A short time ago, my biggest goal in life was to reach California and my aunt. Now, all I want is a chance to tell Luke that I love him and that I don't want to go to San Francisco."

"Very often," Edward whispered close to her ear, "it's the unselfish prayers, such as yours, that are answered the quickest."

The door to Luke's room opened, and everyone turned expectantly. Doc Hawley entered the room calmly and ordered them all to be seated. Amanda's heart raced, and she was only too glad to sink into the closest chair, for her knees no longer felt capable of holding her up.

"First of all, I'd like to thank you all for your patience and silence," he began. "This type of thing is difficult enough without families making it more so by carrying on." He removed his spectacles and held them up to the light. Evidently finding a slight smudge, he began wiping the glass vigorously with his handkerchief.

"I won't try to hide anything from you. Luke's in a serious condition."

Margaret glanced down at her hands briefly, then as if forcing herself, held her head high and spoke calmly: "Exactly what is my son's condition?"

Replacing his glasses and pocketing his handkerchief, he spoke with authority: "There's hardly a place on his body that isn't bruised or lacerated. Luckily, Luke was in good physical shape, and none of these injuries have me worried. There doesn't seem to be any internal bleeding or damage." He rubbed his forehead and studied each face carefully before adding, "It's the head wound that scares me."

"He's not conscious then?" asked Edward.

"No. He may never come out of it."

"When will you know?" Edward asked.

"That's hard to say. I'll be able to tell more tomorrow. A great deal depends on whether his brain was injured, and if so, how seriously. He may never regain consciousness again, or he may surface briefly. . . ." Doc Hawley hesitated, studying his audience carefully. "Then, even if he does come out of it, I can't guarantee he'll be. . . . " Doc looked down at his hands, where he toyed with his gold ring.

"Normal?" Edward finished.

Doc nodded. "Yes. The injury is in a dangerous place."

"We understand. May we see him?" Margaret asked.

"No reason why you can't. He isn't going to see or hear anything for some time. Can't hurt."

"Thank you, Doctor," Margaret said. "Aaron, will you show Doc to a room for the night?"

When Aaron returned, Edward stood before the family. "We will take turns seeing Luke, but I want Amanda to be the one sitting up with him—at least for now—if that's all right with everyone. She has a special prayer that needs to be answered, and I know if we give God the opportunity, it will be."

"It's fine with me," said Robert. "He'd rather wake up to her anyway. He'll know she's there. That will bring him out of it fast," he winked at Amanda.

"Love is a strong emotion," said Margaret, "and I believe it can do wonders—especially when accompanied by prayer."

"What about the girls?" asked Jared. "Shouldn't one of us ride and get them?"

"Oh, dear!" Margaret's hands flew to her face. "Sarah's due any day. Must we?"

"Sarah's tough, like you, Mother," said Aaron. "She can handle it."

"All right, but she must be told tactfully. You'll do it, Aaron? I know you'll handle it well."

"Yes, Mother. I'll get Elvira and Emily, too."

"Then," Edward said, standing, "you go in and see Luke first."

When Aaron came out of Luke's room, Stewart walked with him. He somberly and silently took Margaret's arm and escorted her into the darkened room.

Amanda's heart lurched. This was the first time she'd seen Stewart Sterling enter a room without its shaking with his loud laughter and jovial charm. Yet she wondered at the courage of this amazing family. Would she ever have the faith in God and the acceptance of His will that they possessed?

When Amanda's turn came, Stewart escorted her into Luke's room. Sensing his reluctance to leave, she put her hand out to stop him when he turned away.

"Please stay with me," she whispered.

He smiled and nodded. "But you're to sit at his side. I've

heard why, and I approve wholeheartedly." He hugged her lightly. "I'm pleased. I knew you loved him!"

"Pray I get to tell him and he understands," Amanda whispered sitting beside Luke.

Stewart Sterling sat at the foot of the bed, with his head bowed in prayer.

Amanda slowly raised her eyes to look upon Luke, then winced. Doc hadn't exaggerated. There was barely an inch that wasn't bruised or cut. She touched his cheek gently. His nose no longer appeared too long. His outdoorish looks no longer seemed too rugged. Luke was handsome! Even bruised and battered, he was the handsomest man in the world, in her eyes.

Remembering his boyish grin and twinkling mischievous eyes, this time it was she who scooped the hair from his forehead.

"I love you, Luke Sterling," she said positively. Amanda repeated those words over and over throughout the night.

16

Stewart snored lightly as he sat upright, with his head cocked at an angle, almost resting on his shoulder. Amanda smiled. It had been a long night. She watched the first light of dawn peek into the window. Squeezing Luke's hand, as she had every few moments, she repeated the words she'd spoken all night. "I love you, Luke Sterling."

She looked at Stewart for his usual response to her words. He sat up straight, smiled at her, blinked his weary eyes several times, and dozed off again.

There was never a response. Only once Amanda had thought she'd seen his eyelids flutter briefly. Then she wondered if they had really moved, or was she merely tired and imagining things?

With her free hand she touched his cheek lightly. "I love you, Luke Sterling."

No matter how many times she'd kissed his cheek in the past hours, the desire remained stronger than ever. She touched her lips to his cheek. Something was different! She drew back quickly and touched her lips to be sure. They were wet! She touched his cheek. It was wet! She looked at the ceiling, though she knew not why, for it wasn't raining, and the wetness was too warm to be a leaky roof! She examined his cheek closely. There was a path running from his eye to the wet spot. A tear! Her heart raced frantically. Was that a good sign?

"I love you, Luke Sterling." She spoke louder than she had before. When Stewart jerked awake, she caught his attention before he fell asleep again. "Mr. Sterling, look! A tear! Luke can hear me, I know he can!"

Stewart raced to the bedside and touched the cheek closest to Amanda, then examined the other side.

"Look, this side is wet, too!" he exclaimed.

"That's a good sign, isn't it?" she asked.

"I think so." Stewart beamed at her. "Keep talking to him. I think he can hear us." He put his mouth near his son's ear, "I love you, Son. Please come back to us!"

The room was now flooded with early-morning sunlight. With her hands still beneath his, Amanda continued talking to Luke. "I love you, Luke Sterling. I have for a long time. I didn't recognize it and then couldn't admit it." She kissed his cheek. "I love you. I don't want to go to San Francisco. I never want to leave you or this family. I love you, Luke."

When Margaret tiptoed in, Stewart and Amanda told her about Luke's tears. She hugged them both and thanked God. She sent them both out to the dining room for breakfast, while she sat and talked to Luke.

Elvira, Sarah, and Emily arrived with Aaron. Amanda felt awkward meeting Sarah under such adverse conditions, but was amazed at how like Margaret she was. Even heavy with child, she held herself with confidence, courage, and undoubting faith in God.

Elvira also appeared strong; only Emily cried and whimpered as Amanda had. Edward comforted her.

When Doc Hawley came in for breakfast, Stewart immediately relayed the news of Luke's tears.

"*Is* it a good sign, Doc?" Stewart asked.

Doc scratched his head and looked thoughtful. "Hmm-m-m. It certainly isn't a negative one! I can't promise it means he'll recover, mind you. It depends on why the tears fell. Did he respond to Amanda's words? Or is his body merely functioning automatically?"

"What do you mean, Doc?" Luke's father asked.

"I mean his physical body is operating normally. A tear or two could just fall on its own without meaning he produced it by brain action."

"You mean," Stewart asked, "that if it were warm in his room, he'd perspire. If his bladder were full, he'd excrete, and so forth?"

The doctor nodded, pouring himself coffee. "However, it is possible he is responding. I just don't want you to build false hope."

"Thank you, Doc," Stewart said, slapping him lightly on the back.

"I think, young lady," Doc looked at Amanda's tired face, 'that you need some sleep."

"B-but Luke . . . ," she started.

"I'm going in to examine him. I want you to get some rest." He bent close so only she could hear his words. "It's all right, he'll be fine until you return. Just between you and me, I think he heard you and responded in the only way he could. Your message has been received."

Amanda smiled and hugged the elderly doctor. She followed his orders and slept for most of the day.

That evening she again sat beside Luke, holding his hand and talking to him. The rest of the family took turns sitting at the foot of his bed, watching Amanda love Luke back to awareness.

"I love you, Luke Sterling," Amanda stated with as much feeling as she had the first time. "I love you." She was about to squeeze his hand when a slight movement stopped her. Had he moved his fingers? Had he tried to squeeze her hand? Again she felt the slight pressure on her hand. She looked at Robert, who was sitting at the foot of the bed, gazing idly out the window.

"Robert, he's trying to squeeze my hand, ' she cried.

Robert sprang to her side. Amanda put Robert's hand where hers had been.

"He did! I felt it!" Robert exclaimed. "It was weak, but wonderful." He patted his brother's arm. "You're going to make it. I know you are!"

For three days, on and off, the family felt Luke's weak hand movements. On the fourth day after the accident, Amanda was called from her daytime sleep to Luke's side.

"Come quickly, Amanda," Margaret shook her shoulder 'Luke is calling your name!"

While Amanda hastily dressed, Margaret filled in the details. "First, he opened his eyes," she said excitedly. 'Then he looked around the room, closed them again, and fell back asleep. An hour or so later he opened them again and called for you. Doc thought it wise to send for you as soon as possible."

Although the day was sunny, the room was dim, for someone had closed the gingham curtains. Amanda took her usual place beside Luke, while Mr. and Mrs. Sterling, Doc Hawley, Robert, and Aaron looked on from the foot of Luke's bed.

Picking up Luke s hand, Amanda brought it to her lips and kissed it. "I love you, Luke Sterling." There was no response. With a worried look, Amanda turned to Doc Hawley.

Doc smiled. "He's fallen asleep. Don't worry, he'll come around again." He winked. "This time you'll be there for him."

Amanda returned his smile and made herself comfortable in the chair beside Luke. Leaning over, she kissed his cheek gently. As she pulled away, she saw his eyelids flicker. She squeezed his hand. She gasped slightly when both his eyes opened and focused on her.

"Amanda?" he asked weakly.

"Yes! I'm here, Luke," she cried softly. "I love you," she said clearly and boldly. If he never heard another word on earth, she knew he'd heard those three important ones, for he smiled slightly and squeezed her hand weakly.

He wet his lips with his tongue, then whispered, "And I love you."

"Oh, Luke!" she cried, hugging him. "Please don't die! I need you!"

He smiled weakly and moved his eyes toward the foot of the bed. He smiled at his father. "I'm keeping her," he whispered.

Thanksgiving was a gala affair at the Sterling ranch, especially this year. They had much to be thankful for. Not only was Luke recovering rapidly, but Sarah's baby girl had made her debut, healthy and robust. The house filled with sweet smells of home cooking, and the true spirit of love and happiness. Each person seated at the long dining table had a turn giving his or her personal thankfulness to God. When Amanda's turn came, she thanked God for giving her such a wonderful family to help her get over the loss of her own.

After Thanksgiving the Sterlings began preparing for Christmas with zest and exuberance. Amanda couldn't help but get caught up in the excitement and festivities. Luke was up and about, but still not able to carry out his usual chores. He and Amanda had, since the day he regained consciousness, enjoyed a loving relationship. Though there had been no more talk of love or the future, they spoke with hand squeezes, smiles, and special looks.

Amanda smiled at her reflection in the large oval mirror in Celia's bedroom, which was now her room. The emerald taffeta brought out the green in her eyes beautifully.

Margaret knocked and peeked in. "Oh, Amanda! Didn't I tell you that dress would be perfect?" Closing the door silently, she stood gazing at her in awe.

"Are you sure the neckline isn't too low?" Amanda asked.

Margaret shook her head. "Not in the least. Turn around. Let me see the back."

Amanda spun around gracefully.

Margaret held Amanda at arm's length. "Will you let me put just a dab of powder on the end of your nose?"

"It is shiny, isn't it?" Amanda sat before the dressing table and allowed Luke's mother to powder her nose. "Will you put my hair up the same way you did for Thanksgiving?" she asked.

"Oh, no!" Margaret's eyes twinkled. "Christmas Eve calls for something even more spectacular." Margaret brushed Amanda's thick, wavy hair briskly. "I can't wait for Luke to see you."

Margaret noticed Amanda's smile fade. "What's wrong? Is there a problem between you two?"

Amanda bit her lip. "We seem to still have difficulty communicating. I found it so easy to tell him I loved him when I thought he might die. Now that he's recovered I find myself tongue-tied again."

"But you seem so much closer."

"Yes, we are. We can convey our feelings, but not with words."

"I suppose," Margaret spoke with several hairpins in her mouth, "it would be easier if there weren't always family around. We haven't been too considerate. We should have left you two alone more. How thoughtless! I'll arrange more privacy for you and Luke."

Amanda spoke to Margaret's reflection in the mirror. "Has he said anything more to you about sending me on that ship to California?" Amanda thought Luke's mother paled somewhat at her question. *Why do they all look so guilty whenever I mention my trip to San Francisco? Why do none of them ever ask me not to go?*

After several moments' hesitation Margaret answered her. "He hasn't mentioned it lately. But let's not even talk about it until after Christmas. This is Christmas Eve! I want you to forget about the trip and enjoy your first Christmas at the SOS Ranch." Margaret stood back and exclaimed, "A masterpiece!"

Amanda picked up the hand mirror and looked at her hairdo. Margaret had pulled the thick curls back and up to cascade down her back and shoulders with a bounce, leaving just a few wisps of hair at her cheeks. "It's lovely, Margaret. Thank you!"

"Your hair is a joy to work with." Margaret walked to the door and opened it. "Now, let's join the others. I can't wait to see Luke's face when he sees you." In a whisper, she added, "And I'll see that you two get more time alone."

Luke's eyes lit up brighter than the candles on the Christmas tree when Amanda walked into the living room with Margaret. His mother escorted her to Luke's side, where she released Amanda's arm and tucked it securely under Luke's.

After telling Amanda how beautiful she looked, Luke was silent. Yet his eyes continued speaking loudly and clearly. Amanda's eyes answered with a loving twinkle.

When the Christmas Eve dinner was over and Edward had conducted devotions, they returned to the living room for coffee. Seated at the upright piano, Elvira played one Christmas song after another, while the large, decorated pine tree blinked and winked at them all from its stand in the corner.

True to her word, Margaret found a way to give Amanda and Luke a few moments alone. She suggested they all go into the kitchen and present Annie with her gift tonight, since she would be spending Christmas Day with family in Laredo. When Luke and Amanda stood to join them, Margaret waved them back down and winked meaningfully.

Blushing at Margaret's obviousness, Amanda smiled shyly at Luke.

Luke smiled with a twinkle in his eyes. "We usually open our gifts on Christmas morning, but I'd like to make an exception this year and give you one gift now, while we're alone. Is that all right with you?"

Amanda nodded. She felt her cheeks burn with excitement.

Luke drew an envelope from his breast pocket. He gave her his best boyish grin before kissing her lips gently, then firmly with feeling. Amanda's arms went around his neck automatically as she returned his kiss.

Luke ended the kiss reluctantly. He smiled again. "Well, actually two gifts tonight—if you want to count that one!"

Amanda rubbed his cheek with her hand. "Your recovery was my gift."

"Merry Christmas, sweetheart," he said, handing her a large white envelope

Amanda carefully opened the envelope and pulled out a thick parchmentlike paper Unfolding it, she scanned the careful writing hurriedly. She saw the words *passage, ship,* and *San Francisco* and gasped, throwing the paper into her lap. Tears overflowed from her eyes and ran down her cheeks. "Oh! Luke! How could you!"

"Amanda, you look disappointed with your gift." Luke's face was serious, yet his eyes twinkled mischievously "You do still want to go, don't you?"

She searched his eyes for the meaning of the situation, but found nothing she could identify. *How can he send me away?* she thought, sobbing. *He doesn't even seem to care!*

"Don't you?" he asked again. "Isn't Aunt Hattie waiting for you?"

Amanda nodded tearfully.

"Are those tears of joy or remorse?" Luke tilted her chin up so that their eyes met.

"Oh, Luke!" she cried, wrapping her arms around his neck. "I don't want to go anymore. Didn't you hear me tell you that when you were hurt? Didn't you hear me say I loved you and no longer cared about San Francisco? I can't bear to leave you!"

"Oh, sweetheart!" he cried, squeezing her to him. "I longed to hear you say it again. I was afraid you'd only said that because you thought I was dying. I wondered if you had truly meant it."

He drew back and gazed at her lovingly. "I love you, too. I have for a long, long time." He wiped at her tears with his finger. "Read the paper carefully, out loud."

Hating to take her eyes from his, Amanda finally looked down at the paper and read slowly:

This ticket books passage for two on January 30, 1851, on the ship *Yellow Rose*, bound for San Francisco. Sleeping quarters will be the bridal suite, and the ship sails promptly at dawn. Merry Christmas. Signed, Stewart and Margaret Sterling, who shall hereafter be called Mom and Dad.

"Oh, Luke!" Amanda exclaimed. "How lovely!"

"Wait!" Luke laughed. "I can't let Mom and Dad do all my work for me." He slipped down upon his knees, looked up at her lovingly and whispered, "Will you marry me?"

"Yes!" she whispered back. "I thought you'd never ask!"